THE TEMPTING

OF

PESCARA

BY

CONRAD FERDINAND MEYER

TRANSLATED FROM THE GERMAN

BY

MRS. CLARA BELL

HOWARD FERTIG

NEW YORK · 1975

Library of Congress Cataloging in Publication Data
Meyer, Conrad Ferdinand, 1825-1898.
 The tempting of Pescara.
 Translation of Die Versuchung des Pescara.
 Reprint of the 1890 ed. published by
W. S. Gottsberger, New York.
 1. Pescara, Ferdinando Francesco d'Avalos,
marchese di, 1489-1525—Fiction. I. Title.
PZ3.M574Te6 [PT2432]   833'.7   75-4902

THE TEMPTING

OF

PESCARA

BY

CONRAD FERDINAND MEYER

TRANSLATED FROM THE GERMAN

BY

Mrs. CLARA BELL

REVISED AND CORRECTED IN THE UNITED STATES

NEW YORK
W. S. GOTTSBERGER & CO. PUBLISHERS
11 MURRAY STREET
1890

Facsimile of the title page of the original edition.

THIS TRANSLATION WAS MADE EXPRESSLY FOR THE PUBLISHERS

THE TEMPTING OF PESCARA.

CHAPTER I.

IN a room in the castle of Milan sat its young
Duke Sforza over the accounts of his exchequer.
His chancellor was at his side explaining the items as
he slipped his finger down the page.

"A fearful total!" sighed the duke, horrified at the
sum which had been swallowed up by the rapidly-
constructed fortifications. "So many drops of sweat
wrung from my poor Lombards!" And to escape the
sight of the sinister columns he raised his melancholy
eyes to the wall which was covered with brightly-tinted
frescoes. To the left of the door Bacchus held high
festival with his mythological rabble, and to the right, as
a companion subject, the Feeding of the Multitude had
been depicted by a facile but irreverent hand with a
thoughtless indifference to the sacredness of the story
that verged on ribaldry. The Divine Shepherd sat on
high, so small as to be scarcely visible while the fore-
ground was occupied by a jovial crowd, in mien and

dress not unlike a troop of Lombard reapers at their
mid-day meal, displaying all the symptoms of a healthy
appetite with laughable realism.

The duke's eyes — and those of his ever-watchful
counsellor — fell on a romping girl with a large basket
on her arm — intended no doubt to contain the gathered fragments — sitting in the embrace of a youth who
was holding up a broiled fish into which she had set her
dazzling white teeth.

"They, at any rate, are not yet in want of food,"
said the chancellor in jest with mischief in his eye.

A sad smile passed over the duke's thin lips and
vanished again.

"Why should we build fortifications?" he said,
returning to the subject of his troubles. "It is a foolish business. Pescara, the great captain, will soon
sweep them away and make me pay the cost of the
war too. — Listen, Girolamo," and he drew up his
slender figure, "leave me in peace, with your perpetual
secret treaties and articles, you indefatigable scribbler.
I will have no more of them. You are bringing me
and my Lombards to ruin, you scourge of Heaven! I
will not be faithless to the emperor; he is my suzerain.
And I will let myself be flayed by his hellish Spaniards
rather than be urged on and betrayed by my new
allies." He threw himself back in his arm-chair with a
gesture of self-abandonment, and stretching out his

thin legs he exclaimed: "I will marry a cousin or a
sister of the emperor! You can arrange that if you
are half as great a statesman as you fancy yourself."

The chancellor burst into a loud fit of laughter.

"You may well laugh, Girolamo. You always fall
on your feet like a cat however steep the roof you roll
down; but I get broken to pieces. I and my dukedom are melting away in the witches' broth that is
brewed in your brain. — Miserere! A league with the
Holy Pontiff, with Saint Mark's, with the Fleurs de lis!
A disastrous climax! A most unholy trinity! No
one trusts the pope further than he can see him —
neither I nor any other man. He is a Medici! Saint
Mark, my natural enemy and my neighbour, is the
most implacable of saints. And to these add France,
which left my father to rot in a dungeon, and kept my
poor brother Max — whom you sold, you wretch, a
pensioner in Paris."

The lad's mobile features assumed an expression of
horror, as though he saw the torch of his race slowly
dying out. A tear trickled down his thin cheek.

The chancellor stroked his head with paternal kindness.

"Do not be foolish, Francesco," he said. "I sold
Max? Never. It was the logic of fate that made
him surrender after the rout of the Swiss. I agreed as
to his pension with King Francis and bargained that it

should be a handsome one. He himself saw that I meant well by him, and thanked me for it. He is a philosopher who looks down on the world from high ground I tell you; and when he mounted his horse to ride off from hence, he spoke words of wisdom with his foot in the stirrup. 'Thank God,' said he, 'I have nothing more to do with the heavy-fisted Swiss, the emperor's long fingers' — he meant his late lamented majesty Francesco — and the hypocritical thieving Spaniards. — Max had not the art of looking like an Italian prince, so fat and dirty as he is. Your appearance is a very different thing, my little Francesco; there is something princely about you when you hold yourself up; and you have the gift of speech, too, which you inherit from your incomparable father the Moor. I tell you, the day will come when you will be the wisest and greatest prince in all Italy."

The young duke looked doubtfully at his minister.

"Unless you sell me first," he said with a smile, "and knock down my appanage to the highest bidder."

Morone, who was now standing in front of him, a dark figure in his long, black lawyer's robes, replied affectionately: "My sweet Francesco, I will never do anything to hurt you. Why, you know how fond I am of you! You shall be and remain Duke of Milan as surely as my name is Morone. But you must be a good boy and learn to see what is best for your interests."

"But you have not given me a single good reason in favour of your brand-new league! And once for all I will not rebel against my liege lord; it is both wrong and dangerous."

With perfect presence of mind the chancellor, whose imagination supplied him with every form of dissimulation and disguise, hit upon a sufficiently life-like and effectual mask to hold up before his sensitive young master and give him a wholesome fright.

"Francino," said he, "the emperor is to you a locked door. Have you not written to him the most touching letters and he has never answered them? He is but a youth, lost in the distance, and — as they say — no more than a yielding wax puppet in the hands of his Burgundian courtiers. In that you are his superior, for you judge for yourself. In Madrid it is Bourbon who makes rain and shine, the spendthrift constable, who scatters money broadcast, and whose fidelity is above suspicion since he has betrayed his King Francis and is condemned to all eternity to serve the emperor. — Now Bourbon wants Milan; your fief would just suit him. He is a Gonzaga on his mother's side and aims at an Italian throne. Why is it that the emperor cannot make up his mind to grant you the fief when you have paid him thousands? Because he

is keeping your Milan for Bourbon, — I will stake my
life on it. — Bourbon is sure of his game; not long
since, when you sent me to the imperial camp he
almost smothered me with his embraces and even
pressed a purse upon me to prepare me for the pro-
pitious moment. For we are old acquaintances, you
know, from the time of the French dominion."

This was a mixture of truth and falsehood: the
Constable de Bourbon, in a mad drunken mood, had
paid his guest for some choice jest with a princely gift.

"And you took it — wretch!" whimpered the
miserable young duke.

"With the easiest conscience," replied Morone flip-
pantly. "Do you not know, Francesco, what the
casuists teach us: that a woman may accept everything that is offered her so long as she preserves her
virtue? It is equally true for a minister, and enables
me in these hard times to get on occasionally without
claiming my salary. And you may buy a good picture
with the money one day, Francesco; you must have
your little creditable pleasures."

Sforza had turned pale. The hideous image of
Bourbon in his castle, ruling his dominions — of which
indeed he had already held possession for some years,
as French viceroy, before his famous act of treason —
was too much for the lad.

"I always felt it, and the idea haunts me," he said

lamentably.   "Yes, Bourbon wants to have Milan. —
Save me Girolamo; join the league — at once — without delay, or we are lost."

He sprang up and clutched the chancellor by the
arm.

Morone calmly replied: "Nay, there is no such
hurry; however, we may do something towards it this
very day perhaps.   It just happens that yesterday his
excellency Nasi — not Orazio but handsome Lelio —
came to stay with our friend Lolli, the money-changer,
and by a happy chance Guicciardini, too, has arrived,
and he is in favour at the Vatican in spite of his
prickles.   We can talk to these two discreet men, and
I have invited both the Venetian and the Florentine to
supper with you, for I know you like a pleasant chat
and entertaining company."

"What a base, and shameful conspiracy!" cried the
vacillating duke.

"And another person, too, is come here — rode
into the town at daybreak.   He has announced his
purpose of waiting on you at three in the afternoon;
he must sleep first."

"Another — what another?" the lad shuddered.

"Bourbon."

"A plague on the white-faced traitor!" cried Sforza.
"What does he want here?"

"That, he himself will tell you. Hark! The cathedral bell is tolling for vespers."

"You must receive him!" entreated the duke and he tried to escape through a door. But Morone led him back to his seat: " I must beg your highness. — It will soon be over. When the constable comes in rise with dignity and receive him standing. That will shorten matters." He took up a cloak which hung over the back of the chair and threw it round his young master, who, by degrees fighting down his panic, assumed a princely demeanour, drawing up his stately figure and summoning all his natural dignity.

The chancellor meanwhile went to the window below which lay the castle quadrangle, and beyond it the foundation of the newly-planned ramparts.

" On my word!" he exclaimed. " There is the gallant constable, ten yards in front of his suite, calmly sketching our new fortifications in his pocket-book! I will go and bid him in."

Morone presently returned, conducting the famous traitor, a tall slight man with a haughty colourless face, finely-cut features and striking dark eyes — a sinister but impressive personage, who bowed with courtly respect to the duke. Sforza gazed at him timidly.

" Your highness," said Charles de Bourbon, " I do you due homage, and crave an audience for a message from his imperial majesty."

Duke Francesco answered with much dignity that he was ready to listen with respect to the commands of his liege suzerain, but then his legs failed him and he sank into his chair.

When the constable saw the duke seated he, too, looked round for a chair, or at any rate a stool. There was nothing of the kind to be seen and no page in the room. So he flung his rich cloak on the marble floor at the duke's feet and lay down on it in an easy attitude, leaning on his left arm while his right hand rested on his hip.

" By your highness' leave. . . ." he said.

Since his act of desertion Charles de Bourbon had lived in a scorching and consuming atmosphere of hatred of himself. No one, not the most privileged of his peers, would have dared to remind the proud man of his deed, even by a hint, or to allow him to guess at the unanimous verdict of public judgment; but he knew it, and his own corroborated it. He had the deepest contempt for all mankind, beginning with himself, but he was perfect master of himself and no one was more guileless in his demeanour or more colourless in his talk, never permitting himself or others the least irony or scorn, or even the slightest allusion to it. Only, at rare intervals, a demoniacal witticism or a cynical jest revealed the state of his soul, like a flare of light suddenly flashing up from the earth.

After a minute's reflection he began his speech in a pleasant voice, slightly turning his head: " I must beg your highness not to visit on me anything that may be unwelcome in the message I bring. My own personality counts for nothing; I only have to inform your highness of his imperial majesty's determination as formed in council with his ministers, after consulting with his three Italian generals: Pescara, Leyva and your humble servant."

" How is Pescara ?" boldly interposed the chancellor, who was standing at an equal distance from the duke and his visitor. " Is he recovered from his spearwound at Pavia."

" My little friend," the Frenchman replied contemptuously, " let me beg you not to speak unless you are spoken to."

But the duke repeated the question. " Pray," said he, " how is the hero of Pavia ?"

Bourbon bowed politely. " I thank your highness for your gracious enquiry. My distinguished and wellbeloved colleague Ferdinando Avalos, Marchese di Pescara, is quite recovered; he can ride his ten miles without inconvenience." Then he went on: " But allow me, your highness, to come to the point. A bitter dose is best swallowed quickly. — His imperial majesty particularly desires that your highness should take no part in the new league which is concluded or

about to be concluded, between his Holiness, the Kings
of France and of England, and the republic of Saint
Mark."

On this the lord of Milan found words; with well-
assumed amazement and the greatest indignation he
declared that he knew nothing of any such league, and
that he would certainly have been the first, in accord-
ance with his bounden duty to the emperor, to inform
his majesty without delay if any such treason had been
plotted in northern Italy to his knowledge.   And he
laid his hand on his coward's heart.

Bourbon listened politely with bent head, leaving
the young hypocrite to reiterate his lie with fresh complications.   Then he replied very coolly, with the
faintest infusion of contemptuous pity: "Notwithstand-
ing your highness' asseveration I cannot but believe
that you are not accurately informed as to the state of
affairs.   We think it better that you should be.   The
treaty of peace between France and England with evil
intent as regards the emperor is a fact which has come
to us with absolute certainty through the Netherlands.
We are equally well-assured that nothern Italy is arming against us.   And, so far as it is permitted to judge
of the Holy Father, he, too, whom we have spoiled
and humoured, seems to be secretly turning against us.
It is no part of our task to distinguish between what
has been done and what is only plotted; we must be

prepared — that is to say," he added in a low and significant tone, " before the league has found a leader."

Then he formulated his demand : " Your highness must pledge yourself to remain neutral for the space of one month. That is his imperial majesty's express desire. And in earnest of the pledge he requires that you shall disband the Swiss, reduce the Lombard armed force by one-half, put a stop to the construction of all fortifications, and hand over this ingenious gentleman. . . ." and he waved his hand — " to his majesty. If not," and he sprang to his feet as though about to leap on horseback — " if not, on the last day of September, at midnight, not an hour sooner or later, we sound the trumpet and in a few marches are masters of your duchy. It is for your highness to decide."

He bowed and left the room.

When Morone was about to escort him to the gate Bourbon fell into one of his wild fits of gaiety and waved him off with a farcical flourish : " *Adieu, Pantalon, mon ami*," he called over his shoulder.

Morone flew into a rage at this gibe, which seemed to imply that he was altogether unworthy to be taken in earnest : he angrily marched up and down the room, entangling his feet in the envoy's cloak which he had left on the floor. But the young duke caught him by the arm, wailing : " Girolamo, I watched him ! He feels himself master here already. Join them, — at once; this very day! Or that demon will dethrone me!"

The helpless lad was still clinging in the chancellor's embrace when a grey-headed chamberlain bowed before him, and solemnly announced that his highness' supper was served. The two men followed him as he led the way with an air of importance through the suite of apartments. One of these, a small room, having only one door, seemed with its moss-green velvet hangings and four settees to match, to be a retreat contrived for confidential meetings. The duke stopped in amazement in the midst of this room, for on the wall, usually bare, hung a picture which he did not recognize as his own. It had been secretly brought into the palace as a surprise prepared for him by the Margrave of Mantua — as an inscription on the frame informed him. The duke grasped his chancellor's hand and the two men approached the captivating picture with noiseless steps and silent, absorbed admiration: A man and a woman, of the size of life, were playing chess at a marble table. The lady, a bright and radiant creature, magnificently dressed, had laid a hesitating finger on the queen, with a stolen glance of enquiry at her adversary — a warrior of grave and thought-worn aspect, though a smile trembled at the corner of his sternly set lips.

Both the duke and his minister recognized him at once. It was Pescara. And they could guess who the lady was. Who, indeed, could it be but Vittoria Colonna, Pescara's wife and the pride of Italy ? They could not tear themselves away from the picture. They felt that its greatest attraction lay in the noble and tender love which lent its living charm alike to the delicate features of the poetess and the austere face of the soldier; and no less in their youth, for even the scarred and sunburnt Pescara was depicted as a heroic youth.

In fact, at the early age of eighteen they had stood together at the altar, and had since been unfailing in their mutual fidelity through frequent and long separations; she sunk in study of the great Italian poets by the chaste light of her lamp, he poring over maps by the glimmering camp-fire; and then meeting once more in Ischia, the marchese's domain, to them the Isle of the Blest. The loose-minded Italians knew this, and never doubted it, but admired while they smiled.

The two men, as they stood before the picture, felt all the beauty of this union of inspired womanhood with self-mastering manliness. Still, they felt it not in their souls, but with the delicate finger-tips of their artistic sensibilities. They had been standing there some little time when the chamberlain humbly re-

minded them that two guests awaited them in the
antechamber to the dining-room. They went on
through two or three doors, and after brief greeting led
the way to supper.

The party of four sat down to an elegant but not
over-loaded table. During the first exchange of re-
marks the duke glanced at his guests with furtive
curiosity. Three faces could not be more dissimilar.
He knew his chancellor's grotesque ugliness by heart,
it is true; still, it struck him that to-day his fiery eyes
were more restless than usual, and the crisp, coal-black
hair seemed to bristle on his confident brow. By his
side Guicciardini's head looked noble with its manly
outline and an expression of republican pride. The
Venetian, the last of the trio, was a very handsome
man, with long fine hair, slightly satirical eyes, and an
amiable but treacherous smile. Even in colour the
three men were unlike: the chancellor's complexion
was dark olive; the Venetian's was of the transparent
pallor characteristic of the dwellers by the lagoons;
while Guicciardini looked so yellow and bilious that
the duke was prompted to enquire after his health.

"Your highness, I am suffering from jaundice,"
said the Florentine shortly. " My bile has turned, and
no wonder when his Holiness has sent me to his provinces to constitute them a regular State. I am to es-
tablish order where priests have the mastery! — Well,

no more of that or I shall have an attack of fever, in spite of the wholesome air of Milan and the good news from Germany." He pushed away a sweet dish and dressed himself a salad of cucumber with more vinegar than oil.

"News from Germany?" enquired the chancellor.

"Yes, Morone. I have a letter from a trustworthy source. The rebel peasants are put to rout, and better still — Fra Martino himself has denounced them in speech and writing. This rejoices me, and makes me believe in his mission. For, gentlemen, a man who would move the world has two functions : he must fulfil what his times require, but also — and this is his harder task — he must stand like a Titan opposed to the drenching froth of the century and cast behind him the excited or malignant fools who would try to help but who would fain have a hand in his work, but who would overleap the due limits and bring him to shame."

The duke was somewhat disappointed, for he loved war and tumult so long as they raged on the further side of the Alps, and excited his imagination while he remained in safety. But Morone sighed and said with genuine human feeling :

"Terrible things must be doing in Germany !"

"I am sorry for it," replied the Florentine, "but I keep my eye on the great end. Now, after the refractory barons and insurgent peasantry are quelled the princes will lead. The Reformation, or whatever they choose to call it, will be saved."

"And you call yourself a Republican?" said the chancellor sarcastically.

"Not in Germany."

Even handsome Lelio allowed himself a jest: "And you serve his Holiness, Guicciardini?" he lisped out.

Guicciardini, who had no liking for Nasi's sweet smile, and who was made irritable by his jaundice, answered assertively: "Yes, my lords, I do, for my sins. The pope is a Medici and Florence has fallen a prey to his family. But I refuse to be driven forth from my native city, for there is no lot so hard as that of exile, and no greater crime than to fight against the home of one's fathers. His Holiness knows who I am, and takes me as he finds me. I serve him, and he finds nothing in me to complain of. But I will not submit to have my mouth stopped, so I dare to say it, and with satisfaction, here among men who know: Fra Martino has a good cause and he will uphold it."

It was good sport for the young duke and he felt a malicious joy in hearing a servant of his Holiness extol the great German heretic, though he shuddered at his doing so in his presence and under his palace-roof. He signed to the servants, who had just set the fruit on

2

the table, to leave the room, for they were listening to the exciting dialogue with silent attention.

Morone, who had been fidgeting in his seat meanwhile, now defiantly addressed the Florentine with a flash of his dark eyes: " You are a statesman, Guicciardini, and I dabble in such matters myself. Well then, give your reasons for that astounding statement: Brother Martin, you say, is doing good work, and the work will prosper and endure."

Guicciardini calmly emptied his glass while Lelio crumbled a sweet cake; the duke leaned back in his chair as was his wont and Morone sprang eagerly to his feet.

" Do you think, my lords," the Florentine began, " that a child, or even a fool, would tolerate a thing which pretended to remain always the same when it had turned into its very opposite, as for instance a lamb into a wolf or an angel into a fiend. Now, whatever we, in our new culture in Italy, may think of the Sacred Being of whom the pope is the perennial representative, one thing is beyond dispute: His will was one with all goodness and beauty. But think of his successors — the men on whom the office and work of the Nazarene has devolved? — You have only to look at the four who have held it since the beginning of the century: the conspirator who assassinated our good Julian! The shameless trafficker in Divine

pardon! Then the murderer, the atrociously tender-
hearted paterfamilias.   And these are not mythical
inventions, but monsters of flesh and blood looming in
colossal proportions before our very eyes.   And then
the fourth, whom I would distinguish from those three:
Our great Julius — a hero, the war-god Mars, but not
less than the others a glaring contrast to the Heavenly
Founder of all Peace!   Four such renegades in suc-
cession!   It is a perfect mockery of human reason.   It
must end : Either that first Divine example must be
lost in this reeking hell, this flaming forge of weapons ;
or else Brother Martinus must rescue it, and with one
sharp stroke cut off such successors and adminis-
trators."

"That is pleasant!" said the duke, while the chancellor clapped his hands like one demented.

"A sermon worthy of Savonarola!" drawled Lelio,
swallowing a yawn.   "If only we had Fra Martino in
Venice we could put a bit in his mouth and make him
useful; but if he is left to the guidance of his own
German dunderhead, I fear he will sooner or later
follow Fra Girolamo to the stake."

"No," said Guicciardini confidently.   "For his
brave German princes will protect him with their
swords."

"But who is to protect the princes?" asked the
Venetian satirically.

Guicciardini laughed heartily. " The Holy Father,"
he said. " You see my lords this is one of the most
damned elaborate tangles which Chance — or a Better
power — ever brought about in history. Since our
popes have become worldly-minded and possessed a
sovereignty in Italy the tiny sceptre has been dearer to
them than the long pastoral staff. Is not our Holy
Clement on the point of declaring war in due form
with his faithful son, the emperor, merely for the sake
of that little sceptre ?   Now Charles will hardly force
his brave German soldiers to return to the true fold to
please a pope who turns his cannon against them.
And on the other hand: If the heretical German
princes rebel against his imperial majesty and desert
his standard, do you not think that the Holy Father
will be content to leave their souls alone for the
present and quietly make use of their arms ?   And all
this time the tree is spreading and its roots striking
deep."

The duke was growing restless.   The pleasantest
hour of his day was at hand, when he went out to feed
his dogs and hawks with his own hand.

" Well, gentlemen," said he, " this German monk
will never prevent me.   I have seen his portrait: a
heavy peasant head, no neck, high-shouldered, — and
his patron, the elector of Saxony — a beer cask."

Guicciardini crushed the frail glass in his hand and

ground an oath between his teeth. " It is very hot in
this room," he said, and the duke instantly rose. " We
will go into the air," he said. " We meet again, my
lords, after sunset, in the little green room."

He left the room to show the buildings, terraces
and gardens to the Venetian for whom he had taken a
liking. It was still the matchless structure erected by
the last of the Visconti and filled with his bogey
goings-on, the remains of the " castle of joy," where,
lurking like some uncanny demon in an enchanted
palace, he had ruled Italy with masterly skill, and from
whence he had sent away even his favourites as soon
as they fell ill so that death might never knock at
those marble gates.

A great deal of this former splendour had vanished
or been destroyed and wrecked by war, or by the
recent works of fortification. But enough remained to
justify the handsome Venetian's flattering admiration,
and Francesco Sforza passed a few delightful hours in
his company. It was not till they went to the riding-
schools constructed by the Constable de Bourbon
during his governorship of Milan that the young
duke's face clouded, and even then it soon cleared
again. Guicciardini's loud laugh fell on his ear and
he discovered him sitting in his shirt-sleeves in an open
verandah among the Lombard stablemen playing cards
and drinking a sharp wine of the country.

"The pleasures of a Republican!" sneered Sforza.
"He is refreshing himself after sitting in princely company." And Lelio smiled ambiguously as they went
on their way.

The first to find his way to the green drawing-
room, if indeed he had not gone there straight from
the dining-room and not quitted it since, was Girolamo
Morone. He was lost in contemplation of the picture.
For a time he had feasted his enchanted eye on the
beautiful lady, but now he was scrutinizing the counte-
nance of Pescara, and as he read — or fancied — a
meaning in the strongly marked face, his excitement
found utterance in vehement gesticulations and broken
sentences.

"What will your next move be, Pescara?" he muttered, giving words to the arch enquiry in Vittoria's
innocent gaze, while he fiercely knit his own black
brows.

He felt a heavy slap on the shoulder.

"Are you in love with the divine Vittoria, you
booby?" asked Guicciardini with a rough laugh.

"Jesting apart, Guicciardini, what do you think of
that fellow in the red doublet?"

"He looks like an executioner."

"No, no. I mean what do you think of his face?
Is it that of an Italian or of a Spaniard?"

"An excellent mixture, Morone; the vices of both:

false, cruel, avaricious. Just what I have found him, and you yourself have described him so. Do you remember? In Rome, two years since, when that witty rascal Jacob ferried us over the Tiber."

"Did I? Then it was under the mistaken impression of the moment. Men and things change."

"Things — yes; men — no. They may swagger and disguise themselves, but they remain the same. Do not you say so, Duke?" and he turned to Sforza who came in at the moment, followed by the Venetian.

They seated themselves on the four green seats and ·the doors were locked. A glowing evening sky filled the open window.

"My lords," said the duke with much dignity: "How far do your powers extend?"

"Your humble servant is commissioned to sign a seal," said Lelio.

"His Holiness' wisdom is not less desirous of a conclusion," said Guicciardini. "This league has long been his darling project. He places himself at its head, as becomes his eminence, but with the necessary reservations due to the Head of the Church."

"Then the league is an accomplished fact!" cried the duke heartily. "Chancellor, give us your report."

"My lords," said Morone, "from letters I have received, the French regent, by the concurrence of the king now imprisoned at Madrid, promises us a con-

siderable contingent, and at the same time resigns to
his Holiness all claims on Naples and Milan."

"*Optime!*" cried the duke. "And we could have
as many Swiss as we liked, in unlimited number, if
only we had the ducats to jingle in their ears. Could
we not, Morone?"

"That must be seen to," said the other two.

"But, gentlemen," said Morone urgently, "time
presses. Bourbon has been here. Our game is seen
through. The three generals have threatened to take
possession of Milan within a month if we are not prepared to meet them. We must strike, and in order to
strike we must choose a leader, now — at once."

"But that is what we came for," said the other two
again as with one voice.

"The league must have a captain," the chancellor
repeated. "And the choice is tantamount to deciding
the fate of Italy. — Whom can we nominate to defy
Pescara, the greatest captain of our time? Name the
man who is his superior; show me that inspiring
figure. — The epitaph has long been written over our
great warriors Alviano and Trivulzio, and Pavia killed
the rest. Name the man! Where is that strong and
rescuing hand that I may grasp it?"

A melancholy mood had crept over the little party;
the chancellor revelled in the dejection of his colleagues.

"We have Urbino or the Ferrarese," said Nasi; but Guicciardini explained definitively that his Holiness would have nothing to say to the Duke of Ferrara as being a recalcitrant vassal of the Church.

"Let us invite the Duke of Urbino. He is mean-looking and greedy, narrow-minded and eternally dilatory and vacillating; but he is an experienced soldier, and there is no one else," said the Florentine with a scowling brow.

"There is your Giovanni de' Medici, Guicciardini, and in him you would have just such a young dare-devil as your heart seems set on," said the Venetian laughing.

"Are you mocking me, Nasi?" retorted Guicciardini angrily. "Shall a lawless youngster desecrate our patriotic cause, and a foolhardy boy risk the issue of our last struggle on the remote chance of a reckless fight? Urbino will not be our ruin at any rate, though he may spin out the war by waiting for a raging fever or an insurrection of the soldiery to weaken the imperial camp. Let us choose him."

He sighed, and at the same moment turned furiously on the chancellor whom he had detected in the act of commenting on the end of his speech by a despairing gesture. "Give over your grimaces, idiot?" he shouted at him. — "I must crave your highness' pardon for being out of patience — and your highness agrees with me I believe. . . ."

The duke looked at Morone.

"So be it," said Morone, "we agree. But his highness gives unwilling consent to this depressing initiative to our confederation." The duke nodded gloomily. "Nay," the chancellor went on, "he refuses it; his highness withdraws, he cannot take the responsibility of exhausting the last strength of his duchy. He will not take the field, beaten and disheartened beforehand. The league is dissolved! Or we must find a victorious leader."

The other two sat silent and ill-content.

"And I know of one," Morone added.

"You know him?" cried Guicciardini. "By all the devils, out with it! Speak! Whom are we to set in the scale against Pescara?"

"Speak out, Chancellor," the Venetian insisted.

Morone, who had risen from his seat, took a step forward and said in a loud tone: "Whom are we to set in the scale against Pescara? — Why, Pescara himself."

His three companions were petrified with amazement. The duke stared at his astounding minister with wide-open eyes, while Guicciardini and the Venetian each slowly raised a hand to his brow and began to meditate. Both, as shrewd men, easily guessed what Morone would be at. They were the sons of an age in which every kind of treachery and breach of

faith were a matter of every day occurrence. And if
the man in question had been an ordinary condottiere,
one of those royal or plebeian adventurers who sold
their services to the highest bidder, they would have
snatched the base words from the chancellor's lips.
But the captain-general of the Imperial troops! Pescara? Impossible! — And yet, why not Pescara?
And when Morone began again in vehement excitement they drank in his words.

"My lords," he began, "Pescara was born among
us. He never has been in Spain. The fairest woman
in Italy is his wife. He must love Italy. He belongs
to us, and in this fateful hour when we are striving to
use our free arm to release the bound one, we claim
the noblest son of our native land — our only leader in
war. We will go to him, cling to him and beseech
him: Pescara save Italy; lift her up; or she will drag
you with her into the abyss!"

"Enough of rhetoric!" exclaimed Guicciardini.
"A dreamer like you Morone is capable of inventing
and proposing, in some wild frolic of his imagination,
impossibilities which, on closer consideration, prove to
be not totally impossible. But now be quiet, and let
more reasonable folks examine and elaborate what you
have thrown out in the ravings of fever. Do not
behave like a madman, but sit down and let me speak.

"My lords, in a crucial dilemma boldness is the

best and only prudent course. The idea of fighting under the Duke of Urbino rises up before us like a mask without eyes; we all feel that he would slowly paralyze us and bring us to ruin by all the rules of war. Rather let us risk the boldest stroke! So I agree; in my opinion we must try Pescara. If he betrays us into the emperor's hand he can be the ruin of us all; but who knows whether he may not yield to his demon. First of all we must ask ourselves: What is Pescara? — I will tell you: He is a man who calculates very cleverly, carefully weighing every possibility on both sides, and who is accustomed to look below the delusive surface of things at their real worth and force. Could he otherwise have been — as he is — the conqueror at Bicocca and Pavia? If we apply to him, he will at first affect great indignation at the proposal which he has beyond a doubt already conceived of and considered, though merely as an abstract exercise of his restless ingenuity. Then he will meditate long and cautiously as to whether out of the material we offer him — that is to say Italy — an army can be first created, and after that a kingdom and — his price. And as the material is sound though stubborn, and needs a strong hand to mould it, we must offer him the highest price — a crown."

"What crown?" said the duke in alarm.

"A crown, your highness, not a ducal coronet. I

meant that of Naples. It is now in foreign hands and so may be regarded as vacant; and a fief of the Church."

"If we are to distribute crowns," sneered the Venetian, "why should we not offer the mythical dream-crown of united Italy to Pescara?"

"The mythical crown!" — The Florentine's face wore an expression of pain. Then he went on defiantly, forgetting himself and his audience: "The crown of Italy! If Pescara rides at the head of our forces it will float before his eyes, though unnamed. Would indeed that he, the greatest man in our history, could seize and hold that ideal crown which so many a hand — and guilty ones too — has stretched forth to reach! Would that it might become a reality on his head! And," he added boldly, "since for the nonce we have cast off all our usual reserve and are giving expression to our innermost thoughts and wishes, I would have you to know my lords that if Pescara is indeed the predestined man — as he may be — great blessings lie in the womb of time and happy auguries may be read in the stars. If he reconstructs Italy he will rule it too! — But I called you a romancer, Chancellor, and I am romancing more wildly than you. — We must come down from the regions of the unborn to plain fact and ask next: Who will undertake the task of àsking Pescara?"

"I, like Curtius, will fling myself into the gulf," said Morone.

"Very well," said Guicciardini. "You are the very man. Any one else would stand speechless and sink into the earth for shame when he stood before Pescara to speak to him of treason. But you are shameless, and capable of anything. You will carry your cap and bells safely out of difficulties and complications where any one else would be lost. If Pescara refuses he will take you as a buffoon and treat you as a practical joker; if he consents, he will easily detect the gravity and importance of the business under your theatrical manner and comic grimaces. Go then, my son, and try what you can do with Pescara."

The duke, who had sunk into a brown study on his stool was about to call for lights, for it was now dusk and he dreaded the darkness. He saw that matters had come to an unexpected crisis and was alarmed.

"Chancellor," he cried. "You shall not go. I will have nothing to do with that overbearing Pescara. If we secure his help he will begin by occupying my plains, which seem made for war, and my fortresses which command them. And when once he has them he will keep them. Then if he is the loser I shall be the first to pay for it, and shall fall without redemption a prey to the emperor, my suzerain. Oh! I see through your schemes! All of you — even he — "

and he glanced piteously at Morone, " think of nothing
but your Italy, and for me you care just so much. . . ."
and he blew on the back of his hand. " But I am a
prince all the same, and I mean to keep my inher-
itance, my Milan, nothing more than Milan ! You,
Girolamo, shall not go to Pescara. Our home affairs
will suffer; I cannot spare you for an hour."

On this, handsome Lelio spoke : " If your highness persists," he lisped out, " our whole plan will fall
to the ground; in that case I have another to propose.
Since — strangely enough — we are seeking a leader
among the Imperial generals, might we not try whether
Bourbon could not be persuaded to change sides once
more, if we made him a handsome offer ?"

The duke started as if stung.

" When must you start, Girolamo ?" he asked.

" First of all, Chancellor," Guicciardini put in, " I
am charged to conduct you to Rome, to his Holiness.
He would fain be better acquainted with you, for he
has a high opinion of you. He calls you Chancellor
Proteus, and declares that in spite of your crazy-look-
ing eyes you have one of the shrewdest heads in Italy."

" So much the better," remarked the Venetian, " if
only because it postpones the decisive moment when
Girolamo Morone appears as Pescara's tempter. I
should wish to prepare for that moment — to give it a
pretext, a root in public opinion. May I explain myself

fully, my lords ?"   His pale face assumed a determined
look, so far as could be seen in the growing darkness,
and he went on in resolute tones : " The chancellor,
though he startled us no doubt when he uttered his
pregnant suggestion, did not altogether surprise us. —
After the fatal fight at Pavia had brought Italy unarmed to the emperor's feet, public opinion inevitably
sought to set some limits to his menacing omnipotence,
and our league is the natural outcome.   At the same
time public opinion began to consider what reward
was due to Pescara for his triumphant victory and the
capture of a king.   Then, as the emperor's greed and
ingratitude are notorious, public opinion came to the
conclusion that he would fail to satisfy the great
general, who would look to others for his guerdon.
And now public opinion is connecting these two ideas :
Our patriotic union — which is beginning to dawn on
them, and the possibility of a higher prize for Pescara.
Thus his defection will seem probable even before it
takes place.   At the same time it is desirable that this
popular and rational view should assume a convincing
aspect and find expression in words intelligible to all
Italy ; and this can only be done by a practised hand
and a fluent tongue.   Now, quite lately, a gifted
stranger has appeared among us, a very promising
young man whom we may hope to detain in Venice. . . ."

"A fig for your Aretine! He has calumniated me shamefully. . . ."

"A splendid fellow! He called me the greatest prince in Italy!" cried Guicciardini and the duke in a breath.

"I perceive that the man is known here for what he is worth," said Nasi with a smile. "His letters to real or fictitious persons, scattered over thousands of pages, are a power in the world, and influence it widely. I will send him a handsome sum of money, and you will be amazed at the crop of gaudy, poisonous mushrooms that will spring up all over the soil of Italy in a single night: verses, arguments, correspondence, a bacchanalian orgy of whirling and leaping figures — some bare, some decently draped, some threatening, some seductive — all spinning round Pescara and the probability of his treachery — and the beauty of the action. Thus an invincible and universal conviction will grow up which will bring Pescara over to our side, and at the same time — and this is the point — will so entirely and effectually undermine him at the imperial court that he must become a traitor whether he will or no."

"That will not do, Excellency," cried the chancellor out of the darkness. "You are spoiling my game. The liberator of Italy must be perfectly free to choose, and not fall a victim to a diabolical stratagem. . . ."

3

"You are too delightful, Chancellor, with your moral scruples," Guicciardini broke in. "I assure you that my heart rebels, too, and is entirely on the side of the poor entrapped victim. But I silence the Man and act as a Politician. His excellency's proposal is out of all comparison the most atrocious of all that have been put forward this evening, but it is the wisest and the most sure to succeed. The business is really becoming dangerous to Pescara, and his defection looks likely. Now, to work!"

"He is among us listening!" cried the duke in a scream, and they all started violently. Their eyes followed his terror-stricken gaze. The moon had risen, a silver disk, and its rays falling aslant into the little room shone weirdly on the picture of the chess-players. Vittoria's prominent eyes glittered wrathfully as though she were saying: "Do you hear, Pescara?" — And Pescara was as pale as death, with a smile at the corners of his mouth.

CHAPTER II.

IN the broad light window-bay of that noble room in the Vatican on whose walls and panels Raphael immortalized the triumph of the human mind, sat an old

man with large features, and of venerable aspect. He
was speaking with serious mien to a woman who sat at
his feet and whose face, upturned to listen, was
crowned with golden brown tresses. She was not less
beautiful in her warm, living humanity than the con-
ceptions of Justice and Theology as the great Urbino
had embodied them in majestic female loveliness. The
aged pope, bent by years, looked in his flowing white
robes, like a venerable matron, chatting of prudence to
a young wife.

Vittoria could not long have been seated there on
her low stool, for the Holy Father was just enquiring
after the health of her husband, the Marchese di Pescara.

"The wound he got at Pavia no longer troubles
him then?" he said.

"The marchese is quite recovered," replied Vittoria
simply. "The wound in his side is healed as well as
the worse cut on his forehead. He will pay his
respects to your Holiness when he gets the leave of
absence which the emperor, of his grace, has promised
him, and which will bring us together again, in perfect
happiness, in our island home." Her eyes shone with
glad anticipation. "But he himself has refused it for
the present; not for political reasons, for the outlook is
neither brighter nor gloomier than usual — so he
writes; but because he is unwilling to leave the army
just at this juncture. The assassin," she went on with

a smile, " is very busy trying an improved fire-arm and
a new system of manœuvres. He would be glad to
bring them to perfection. So he has bidden me to join
him at his camp at Novara, instead of surprising me
by appearing here in Rome as he at first intended, and
I start to-morrow — not at a snail's pace in my litter,
but on my fiery little Turkish horse. Oh, if I had but
wings! I long to see my lord's scars, for I have not
set eyes on his face since that great fight which has
made him immortal. So, in the joy of my heart, I
hastened to your Holiness, to take leave of you : that
is the purpose of my visit." Vittoria poured it all out
with the bubbling flow of a Roman fountain.

Her frank speech showed his Holiness that Pescara
kept his movements and doings in the same twilight
obscurity as he himself affected; with this difference
however that the more youthful Pescara could rush
forward at the decisive moment like the lightning flash
from a cloud, while Clement would remain undecided,
and angry with himself for hesitating with senile
caution, to seize the right moment. He would sit so
long, sharpening the pencil, as it were, that when he
tried to use it, the point, to his disgust, broke short off.
And now he felt his way softly.

" Did the marchese only ask for leave ?" he said.
" I thought he had begged to be dismissed. Achilles
sits surly in his tent — I was told."

" I know nothing of that, and I do not believe it,
Holy Father," replied Vittoria with a proud shake of
her head.   " Why his dismissal ?"

" Not by reason of any rosy Briseis, Madonna,"
replied Clement irritably, with an ungenial jest. " Only
cheated out of a captive king, and the castles of Sora
and Carpi."

The pope alluded to two well-known facts : The
viceroy of Naples had intervened at Pavia, and by
requiring the king of France to give up his sword had
deprived Pescara of the honour of carrying his illustrious captive to Spain.   And afterwards the emperor
had presented Sora and Carpi to the Colonnas, Vittoria's relations, instead of to his great general who
had likewise cast a covetous eye on those places.

Vittoria coloured angrily.

" Holy Father, you have a mean idea of my husband.   You think of Pescara as a petty mind.   Grant
me leave to depart on my journey and convince myself that your Pescara and mine are not the same.   I
am in haste to find myself in the presence of the true
Pescara."

She rose and stood towering above the pope, but
instantly bent low again, in a humble attitude, craving
his blessing.   He begged her to sit down again and
she obeyed.   Clement felt that he must not lose the
opportunity of persuading Pescara to secede by the

mouth of the wife he loved. He easily perceived that
this was not to be attained through hints and suggestions to the fair Colonna who sat at his feet: either
she would revolt against his half explanations and in-
nuendoes, or she would pass them by unheeded, as
beneath her notice. He must sketch the position in
distinct outlines to this truthful and truth-seeking
nature and place it in a clear light if she was to be in-
duced to consider it. And this was against his usual
practice; he sighed deeply.

However, a way out of it occurred to him not
devoid of ingenuity and cunning: Laying his hand,
with the ring of St. Peter, on a book in blue velvet
binding, with clasps of gold, he asked Vittoria with an
air of simplicity: "Are you writing anything in poetry,
dear daughter? I am a sincere admirer of your muse
because your themes are always good and holy. And
I especially admire it when you ask and answer questions of morality. Still, you have never, in your
sonnets, discussed the most difficult moral problem of
all. Do you know which that is, Vittoria Colonna?"

The lady was not surprised at the Holy Father's
sudden attack, for here she stood on her own ground;
her name was already famous, and scholars and lay-
men alike frequently addressed such questions to her.
She was ready for the fray and drew up her slender
figure, her eyes brightening as she spoke.

" The most difficult moral problem," she said un-
hesitatingly, " is the choice between two supreme
duties."

Now all was plain sailing for his Holiness.

" It is so," he affirmed with theological gravity.
"That is to say apparently supreme, for one of the two is
in fact the higher, or else there would be no moral law
in the world. I beseech God and the saints to aid
you and grant that you may always discern the higher
and prefer it to the lower — you and your husband;
for behold this great and difficult task is at hand for
you both."

Vittoria turned pale at finding a school dilemma
suddenly stinging her to the quick; and the pope
went on in solemn tones: "Listen to me, my daughter!
And all that I have to say to you is said to the marchese as well; to him you must transmit my words.
Understand this: At this hour the Pontifical chair is
divided against the imperial throne, and offers you the
leadership. I do this as sovereign and as Pontiff. As
sovereign : because to-day is the turning point of the
fate of Italy; if we let it slip, we — the Italian princes
— shall fall henceforth for ever, under the yoke of
Spain. Ask whom you will: this is the opinion of all
men of insight. — But as Pontiff also. Should the
primitive idea of the empire take form in the brain of
that mysterious youth, in whose veins the blood of

many nations flows as on his head rest many crowns, all the painful toil of my sainted predecessors will have been in vain, and the Church will be more heavily fettered, more deeply humiliated by the new state craft than ever it was by the iron rule of the fabulous Germanic monsters, the Salier and the Staufen. — These are the facts. Are you indifferent to that which fills Italy with fear and hope ?"

" The marchese will never believe it," said Vittoria with a sudden flush of colour. The pope smiled. " Your Holiness must not forget," she added, " that I am a Colonna — that is to say a Ghibelline."

" You are a Roman, my daughter, and a Christian," corrected Clement.

There was a pause ; then she asked : " And Pescara ?"

" Pescara," replied the pope in a subdued voice, " is my subject rather than the emperor's, for he is a Neapolitan, and I am suzerain of Naples. Do not think, Vittoria, that I am talking idly. How should I do so — I, who am the conscience of the world ? I tell you in all truth : I have examined myself as to my claims on Pescara through sleepless nights and anxious dawns. Nay, mistrusting my own political judgment, I have asked council of the two shrewdest jurisconsults of Italy : Accolti and — hm — another."

The pope discreetly swallowed down the name

that was on the tip of his tongue, for he remembered
in time that this second councillor, the Bishop of
Cervia, had a reputation for shameless corruptibility.

"They both agree," and Clement rapped the blue
velvet book with his heavy ring, "that Pescara, by
strict justice, is mine rather than the emperor's, and
both have suggested to my memory that, in virtue of
my office as holding the keys, I have it in my power,
now that the emperor is my enemy, to release the marchese from his oath to a foe of the Holy See."

Clement had slowly risen to his feet. — "And I
hereby do so," he said with priestly solemnity. "I
release Ferdinand Avalos from the emperor's service,
and nullify his oath of fealty. I appoint the Marchese
di Pescara Gonfaloniere of the Church and General of
the league known as the Holy League, because Christ,
in the person of His Vicar on earth, is at its head."

The pope paused. Then, raising his left hand in
the air over Vittoria's head as though it held a crown,
he added in a distinct voice: "As the guerdon, in
advance, of my Gonfaloniere's services to me and the
Church I crown Ferdinand Avalos King of Naples!"

The young queen who had sunk on her knees,
overcome by amazement, was trembling with joy.
She thought she had really won a crown, and she
received Clement's blessing in silence, her cheeks
burning. Then she rose and left the room with a

steady though rapid step, as if she could not for a moment delay carrying the crown to her husband.

His Holiness, greatly excited, followed her so hastily that he was near losing one of his slippers. He caught her at the door to offer her the blue velvet volume: " For the marchese," he said.

But he saw, just beyond her, Guicciardini and Morone, who perhaps had been listening at the door some few minutes.   Vittoria, with her radiant looks of intense gladness appeared to the chancellor such a marvel of beauty that he almost lost his presence of mind.   But he hastily recollected himself and addressed the pope: " Will your Holiness introduce me, unholy as I am, to the heavenly Vittoria !" on which Clement, clapping him lightly on the shoulder, introduced him in these words: " The Chancellor of Milan — a man of the world on whom the Holy Spirit is beginning to descend !" and then he added for Vittoria's ear: " Morone — Buffone !" *

Vittoria, bewildered with contentment, vanished; while the pope, in his surprise, kept the heavy blue book, for he was still under the excitement of the audacious symbolical ceremony which the sight of the beautiful young woman had betrayed him into.   However, he was now beginning to feel that he had been thrown off his balance; with a wave of the hand he

* Morone, a buffoon.

dismissed his would-be visitors and retired into the painted room.

The Florentine and the Lombard looked at each other for an instant; then Guicciardini, with a laugh, took Morone by the arm and led him down the thickly-carpeted steps into the garden of the Vatican, though, as the day had clouded over black and dark, they had no need to seek the shade of the alleys.

"For my part," said Guicciardini, "1 can get on very well with the old man. Cleverly as he schemes and cautiously as he speaks, he is at heart more passionate and irascible than I am; and at this moment he is greatly excited, for he has been explaining our dangerous secret to Vittoria. You were too much bewitched to notice that he was pressing the volume of Accolti's and Angelo de Cesis' opinions into her hand. Two venal rascals who disguise their perjury with Bible-texts! It is a strong measure, too, for Clement in his old age to venture on so bold and momentous a task; and what is strange is that he is undertaking it in the deepest distrust of himself, without any faith in his star, for he regards himself at heart as ill-omened. And that is bad. — Leo was quite another sort of man, always beaming and triumphant, and therefore always lucky; while his present Holiness always sees the Eternal City plundered by the foe, and those roofs" — and he pointed to the Vatican — "a prey to the flames; he foretold it all to me the other day, quite in the style of the prophet Jeremiah. And yet he is preparing to fight the emperor; and I think the better of him for it, even if his first thought is for Florence. He still has some blood in his veins, and gnashes all the teeth he has left when he thinks of the haughty Spanish nobles lording it in the capitol, as they do in Naples or Brussels. — But what are you dreaming of, Chancellor? Of the lady? — Of course."

"I will speak to that Roman lady like an ancient Roman!" cried Morone.

"Very good. Only take care that in your enthusiasm you do not let your classical Satyr's hoof appear from under your toga. Be discreet, use big words, and nail her fast by her poetic vanity."

"I will nail her fast by the heart!"

"That is to say by the ink-bottle, for a scribbling woman's heart is filled with ink," said the ribald and scandalous Florentine. "But I tell you what, Chancellor: His Holiness is not the only person who loses his nights' rest over our plot. I have not shut an eye this week past. I cannot help trying to make out this Pescara. I do not count in the least on his quarrel with the emperor; they might make it up again any day; — nor yet on his wife's influence. She will be allowed to give him the pope's message, but he will not listen to another word. On the other hand, I have no belief in his feudal attachment. Pescara is not the Cid Campeador, or whatever the Spaniards call their loyal hero; he is too thoroughly an Italian and a man of his time for that. He believes in no right but might, and in no duty for a great man but that of making himself greater, by using all the means of his time to solve the problems of the time. Such as he is he will suit us well. He will inevitably be our prey and we his. And yet — you may laugh at me, Morone — there is something in the air. I scent something concealed or reserved in the man, something fatal or accidental, something physical or an intangible emanation — in short an unseen obstacle which stands in our way, falsifying and nullifying our most careful calculations."

"But if he is what you take him to be," said Morone seriously, "and if the facts are as they seem to be, from what source of mischief can this adverse influence arise?"

"I know not. Only Pescara's reputation is that he can let an attacking foe climb to the top of the wall and then suddenly turn his guns upon him from behind a crushing rampart. What if a blank wall were suddenly to face us in his mind, at the very moment when we fancied we had vanquished him? — But away with such goblin fears; they are nothing but the heat before the storm, the natural oppression and uneasiness which precede every great and perilous undertaking."

A flash of lightning rent the clouds over the Vatican. It stood revealed by white flame, showing the fine proportions of the new architecture. As the thunder rolled by the two men took shelter under a portico, Guicciardini much startled, and wondering what the omen portended, Morone indifferent to the heavens and the signs in the heavens, for he already pictured himself at Vittoria's feet.

The marchesa, in the bewilderment of her agitation, had quitted the Vatican, going down the first flight of stairs she came to and out of one of the side-doors. She had quite forgotten that her litter and attendants were awaiting her in vain at the main entrance; carried away by her ambitious dreams rather than scared by the impending storm, she made her way on foot to her palace in the Piazza degli Apostoli, her dress floating on the air. She walked on, like Tullia, under her usurped crown — not indeed over the body of her father, but over her murdered loyalty; for Colonna's daughter and Pescara's wife was a Neapolitan, and the subject of Charles V., King of Naples.

The pope's symbolic act of coronation had turned her head. Her habits and surroundings, the belief of her century, and the traditional formulas of piety all taught her to regard the Head of the Church, however

degenerate the individual, as the laboratory of the
Divine will and a vessel of supreme counsel; besides,
her own conscious virtue, and yet more her pride in
her husband's high character, would have hindered her
from doubting the Papal prerogative of placing the
crown on the worthiest brow. Thus the arrogant pro-
cedure of the Medicean Pontiff appeared to her, in
spite of a degenerate age, the direct act of God.

The newly-made queen had passed through the
Borgo, crossed the bridge of St. Angelo, and was now
making her way down the Via Diritta as it was then
called, through the tumultuous crowd. They respectfully made way for her, showing no surprise at seeing
the noble lady alone, nor at her swift step, to which
the gust heralding the storm had now lent wings. By
degrees, however, she moderated her pace in the in-
creasingly dense throng, for the street was narrow;
though the strip of sky overhead grew every moment
blacker and more threatening. Then, over the heads
of the people, she caught sight of a party of horsemen.
Some officials of the Spanish Embassy were escorting
Leyva, the imperial general third in command in Lombardy, to an audience at the Vatican, as it would
seem. This man, once a groom, and the son of a
tavern-keeper and a maid-servant, who had risen by
his servile ambition and his iron determination, was
stout in figure, with the face of a bull-dog; a sword-

cut had seamed his forehead, nose and lip. Next to him, on a thoroughbred Andalusian, rode a noble-looking man wrapped in a white cloak. As he passed Vittoria he bent his dark and energetic-looking head, as it seemed in devout admiration ; but he had in fact only bowed before the stone saints in a church hard by.

Whether it were the lurid, stormy effect of light, or the deliberately hostile demeanour of these gentlemen in a city whose triple-crowned sovereign was, as they well knew, a secret traitor to their king — or, again, Vittoria's excited fancy — in the splendour of these chargers and their riders with their arms akimbo, in their way of glancing scornfully over their shoulders at the sons of Romulus, even in the tips of their pointed beards, she saw and felt only the contempt and inso-lence of the incipient Empire of Spain. A feeling of rage and loathing came over her, and deadly hatred surged up in her Roman soul of all these foreign invaders and high-handed adventurers who were ap-propriating both the Old and New Worlds. Why was the youthful emperor king also of that reprobate nation in whose veins ran the blood of Moors and who had poisoned Italy with the race of Borgia. Under all other circumstances the traditions of her family — a Ghibelline race, who for centuries had found their highest advantage in fidelity without fealty to the imperial cause — would have bound her to Charles; but, as it was, No: not to this emperor — not even if he had not been a Spaniard. She could feel no loyalty to this inscrutable youth whom she had never seen — nor any one else in Italy which he had always shunned.

He had indeed written to her after the victory of Pavia, to congratulate her on being the wife of Pescara. But even in that brief letter she fancied she could detect a narrow spirit; what most displeased the young woman's magnanimous spirit was the humility, in her eyes timid and over-righteous, with which the young potentate ascribed all the glory to God and the Saints. Though she herself could thank Heaven, Vittoria held such abasement cheap in a man and a sovereign. Was it not tantamount to a confession that this splendid triumph did not deeply affect the distant monarch; or was it not even a mean way of flouting Pescara's laurels? Yes, that was why he ascribed everything to Heaven! Vittoria was ardently jealous of her husband's fame. — And how ungenerous Charles had been! He had actually refused the great captain, to whom he owed the dominion of Italy, two miserable little Italian towns. Treason to such a man was impossible; it was at most, secession — leaving him to go his own way.

At this moment she was half blinded by the vivid flash which drove the chancellor and Guicciardini

4

under the porticoes of the Vatican; and, just as the
rain came sweeping down, by turning off to the left,
down a side street, she reached the dark entrance and
splendid vestibule of the Pantheon. Without going
any farther into the temple, she leaned against one of
the closely-planted columns, breathing the cooler air.
Standing there, under the shelter of the ancient build-
ing, her mind went back to even remoter antiquity,
whose virtues the facile imagination of her own time
could extol without possessing them, or even under-
standing their single-minded rectitude and austere
practice.   Those high-spirited Lucretias and Cornelias
rose up before her fancy, soaked as it were in antiquity,
and she hailed them as sisters; she herself bore two
names as truly Roman as theirs, and to her, as to those
noble women, feminine pettiness was a thing unknown.
Those simple and proud creatures had been the
mothers of the world's conquerors.   Virgil's grand
words : " *Tu regere imperio*," which she had often repeated to herself ere this, now moved her to tears.
She went into the sanctuary and flung herself on her
knees under the vault fitfully lighted by the storm, and
wringing her hands and praying that Rome and Italy
might never sink into the abyss of slavery.   Her
prayers were addressed to the God of the Christian,
but not less to the Olympian god who thundered
above her — to all who had saving power and grace —

with the strange and yet so natural confusion of creeds which characterizes periods of transition.

When she quitted the Pantheon — and how long she had been kneeling there she knew not — the fickle Italian sky was already bright again, and she went on her way homewards at her usual light and steady pace.

Her thoughts now reverted to Pescara. Her weak woman's arm could not drive out the Spaniards; only he could do it who held a victory in each hand; if only she and circumstances could win him over! Dared she hope it? Had she so much power over him? — And Vittoria was forced to own that, in spite of their long and trustful married life, Pescara's inmost soul was still unknown to her. She knew his features, gestures, most trifling habits by heart. That this reserved man was faithful to her she fully believed — and she was not deceived. She was proud of knowing that he adored her, and cherished her as his greatest treasure, with the utmost tenderness and devotion, and with equal love and respect. In the blissful hours of their brief companionship, constantly broken by his military duties and camp-life, he would cast aside his plans and maps and Livy to gaze at his wife, or to watch with her the blue sea and passing sails. He would play chess with her, and she won. He would ask her to play her lute, and sit listening with closed eyes. He would give her ingenious subjects for her sonnets, and sometimes polish the first sketch of their common ideas and manifold digressions; for he himself once on a time, in the enforced leisure of imprisonment, had written a poem in her honour — and not a bad one for a man of the sword : — the " Triumph of Love."

But young as he was and high as his hopes were, he would never tell his wife the history of his victories; he would neither weary her, he said, nor bespatter her with blood; and a campaign was a long trial of patience which only led to the red pool of the slaughter-house. He never discussed political events either, neither past or imminent; though once indeed he let it escape him that the greatest thing in life was to rule men and things by invisible hands, and that he who had once known it had nothing further to look forward to. Still, he commonly expressed his opinion that politics were a dirty business, and that his wife was never to dip even the tip of her dainty foot into that foul bog.

So Vittoria confessed to herself that Pescara, who saw through everything and was not to be deceived, was himself impenetrable as to his thoughts and beliefs.

Was this just ? Ought there to be any sealed doors and locked chambers for her in her husband's soul ? As to his plans as a general or his schemes as

a statesman she had no curiosity ; but she longed to
know the secrets of his ambitions and his conscience.
And now, when Pescara was standing face to face with
a momentous decision — now she would not allow herself to be shut out of his struggling heart, she would
not be put off with a kiss or a jest — no, she would be
taken into his council and share in his deeds. Had
she not brought him a maiden soul and youthful
purity ? Was she not a Colonna ? Was she not this
day bearing him a crown ? And whether he refused
it or, on the contrary, accepted it at her hands and set
it on his head, she would be his partner in crime or in
heroism, a conscious part and parcel of his reticent
soul. — Ah, if she were but with him now ! Her
heart glowed, her feet tingled with impatience as she
crossed the Piazza degli Apostoli. Here she was met
by a lad in armour who had been waiting for her
return, at the door of her palace.

" I was growing anxious about your highness," he
said, " for your litter and people have long since come
home from the Vatican without you. — However, here
you are, godmother — if I may still give you the title
to which I have been used from childhood, and which,
indeed, I have a right to give you."

She made no reply but went up the steps, scarcely
resting her hand on his offered arm. She could not
refuse so trivial a service whatever her grievance might

be.   For del Guasto — so the youth was called — was
Pescara's nephew and, like him, an Avalos. Vittoria
as a girl of fifteen, had held this boy at the font with
her present husband.   Her father, the great warrior,
Fabrizio Colonna, had arranged this in order to bring
his two favourites together : Pescara, a young officer
under his command, and his own blossoming daughter;
thus enabling the pair to study each other's figure and
face as they stood by the font.   At a later date Vittoria, being childless, had adopted the handsome and
spirited boy who, in his rich baptismal cap, had unconsciously brought about her marriage, and whose
parents died young.   If only he could have remained
a boy !   But as his features lost their childish softness
his soul lost its gentleness.   The delicate profile grew
vulture-like, with the sharp aquiline outline of a bird of
prey, and the ruthless nature which he developed
repelled and revolted Vittoria.   Then Pescara had
taken him with him into the field and, under the guidance of the captain he adored, he became the daring
soldier who, in the battle of Pavia, led the way to
victory by destroying the park-wall ; but he was also
the stern and cruel officer who during the hasty retreat
from Provence in the previous year, had, without a
pang, set fire to a house while a dozen of his men were
still lingering in the cellar, and saw it burnt to the
ground.

But Vittoria had worse than this to charge him with : a crime which roused the woman in her, and now he should be told of it — now that he was in her presence for the first time since its commission.

First she enquired whether he had come from Pescara and what news he brought. He replied that he had orders to escort the marchesa to Novara. He feared that the sight of him was displeasing to her highness, but he could not refuse the duty laid upon him by the general, who would not confide his wife to any but a trusty swordsman. For the highways were as insecure as the state of affairs, and he must entreat the marchesa to be ready very early in the morning; he was in a fever to be back at the camp where a fight might supervene at any moment, and he must not be absent. The Milanese, Venice, and his Holiness vied with each other in declaring their peaceful intentions; so a battle was certainly imminent.

"We have long known," he said, "that it is merely a matter of opportunity. But," and he drew back a step, "I heard something else, something new and portentous in the course of my journey, and I had no need to play the listener. It is as easy to hear in the inns and villages as the fountain in the market-place. Of course I was travelling under a feigned name and with only one servant."

He paused, looking up with glittering eyes as

though he were watching the exciting course of a
chase, or of an ambush stealing through the pale
moonlight.

"Speak, Don Juan," Vittoria murmured.

"From you, madonna, who have just come from
the Vatican, there can be no secrets; — and this, as I
said, is not a secret, but public rumour — a malicious,
and vengeful chuckle, a hardly repressed shout of
triumph throughout Italy, a general and patriotic
declaration and incitement — and I am in the greatest
haste to report it to the general.   For he knows
nothing of it as yet — so far as I know," he added suspiciously.

Vittoria turned pale.   "What is this rumour ?" she
asked anxiously.   "And whom does it concern ?   Not
Pescara ?"

"Yes, Pescara.   His name is on every lip.   They
say," and he lowered his voice, "that the general is
about to break with the emperor and is in treaty with
his Holiness and the Italian powers."

Vittoria was startled by the ardent and sensual
expression of the youth's face.   "And Pescara. . . ."
she said vaguely.

"How I envy him !" said Juan pensively.   "What
an excitement, what joy for him !   Italy has flung
herself into his arms ; he can caress her, subjugate her
and throw her aside — Oh ! he will play with her as a

cat plays with a mouse!" and he made a clutching gesture of his right hand.

A fire of rage blazed up in the daughter of the Colonnas.

"Wretch!" she exclaimed. "Did I ask you what Pescara would do? Are you the man to divine his thoughts? Have I given you leave to guess and hint at them? — Like a cat with a mouse — horrible! As you played with Giulia, you dishonourable villain!"

Giulia was the daughter of a noble house of Novara and the granddaughter of Numa Dati, a famous physician who had healed Pescara of a spear-wound. Del Guasto, who had been quartered in the physician's house, had seduced the young girl and then changed his residence. The victim, overwhelmed with shame had hidden from her grandfather's unsuspecting face in a Roman convent, and had implored Vittoria, on her knees, to have pity on her and use her influence to repair the disgrace.

When the lady called him a dishonourable villain Don Juan bit his lips.

"Gently, madam," he said. "Weigh your words. I·am not dishonourable. But I should have been if I had not deserted Giulia. I do not speak of the gulf that separates an Avalos from a Dati, but simply of the fact that I, like every other man, decline to wed a bride with a stain on her.

Vittoria's humane soul revolted: "It was you your-self who brought the hapless girl to ruin by your caresses and vows — nay, by deliberate falsehood and perjury perhaps. — Was it not? Can you deny it?"

"I do not deny it," he replied, "but it was by right of war, for there is war between man's desires and woman's innocence. I tempted her — yes. But why did she not resist? Why did she yield? Why do you accuse me because she was weak, and I now scorn her and cast her off?"

Vittoria was petrified with horror. "Ruthless wretch!" she gasped.

"Madonna," said the young man, to cut the matter short, "this is a painful subject and you hurt me deeply. I propose an appeal to a higher tribunal. When we reach Novara we will go before the general and you shall accuse me. I will defend myself, and the marchese, who knows the world and its code, will, as I believe, acquit me. — Now, madam, I leave you. I have still to wait on certain persons, for in these troubled times I dare not be answerable for your safety without powerful protectors." He bowed and quitted her with his head held high.

Vittoria turned away in wrath and passed through the opposite door; she needed fresh air, and went out into the garden. The last light of day was fading as

she stepped forth into the parterre behind the palace,
enclosed with high walls, and full of laurels and
myrtles just refreshed by the evening's rain which still
dripped from their leaves. She made her way to the
casino at the bottom of the garden.

The pale light was still sufficient to enable her to
read, though with some difficulty, the New Testament
which she had taken up on her way through the
library, and which she now opened before her as she
sat with her hot brow resting on her clasped hands.
But her mind was full of Giulia's fate, and of Pescara's
greater destiny, and her eye ran vacantly over the page
as she took deep breaths of the reviving air. After a
while her thoughts began to follow what she read: It
was the history of the threefold temptation of the
Lord in the Desert; she read it with the eye of
memory rather than of the body, having known it by
heart from her infancy.

In fancy she saw the Devil standing before the
Saviour, who answered the tempter's sophistry with the
simple words of faith and obedience. Then, as the
Evil One pressed Him more closely, the Son of Man
pointed to his left side, which the spear would pierce
by and bye. — Gradually the white robe appeared to
turn to glittering armour and the gentle hand put on a
glove of mail; it was Pescara, now, who laid his hand
on the wound she could still discern; while the Devil

wore a long black lawyer's gown and jerked as he moved, like a merry-andrew.

The picture was under her eyes on the open page.

Annoyed by the trick of her senses she shook herself and looked up.

"Who are you, and what do you want?" she exclaimed in amazement; and a dark figure in front of her replied : "I am Girolamo Morone, and have come to speak with Vittoria Colonna."

Vittoria remembered the Pope's introduction that afternoon, and she now also perceived the servant who had led Morone hither. The man lighted a chandelier that hung above his mistress' head, placed a seat for the chancellor and left them while the marchesa contemplated her belated visitor's ugly but powerful face, which inspired her with no aversion.

"You have come to seek me at a late hour," she said. "But no doubt you bring me a message for my lord, Pescara, whom I rejoin to-morrow, starting very early."

"I, myself, hope to stand in Pescara's presence before long," replied Morone. "And it is not of him that I wish to speak but only of Vittoria Colonna whom I revere and worship with all Italy, as a divine being, but whom I nevertheless have a quarrel with, and must accuse."

"And who are you that you dare to speak so to

me?" was the question that rose to the marchesa's lips; but she asked with hasty warmth: "Of what do you accuse me? Of what am I guilty, Morone?"

"Of burying your fair and inspiring face in scrolls and books, of living among shadows and myths! Of hating the first Caesar and doing homage to the last, of bewailing the fate of Troy and forgetting your own people, of suffering under Prometheus' chains and never feeling the fetters of Italy! — Three women forged those fetters."

"Which three?" she asked.

"The first was Beatrice Este. When her husband, the Moor, kissed her blooming lips she whispered to him that a diadem would become her yellow tresses; the Moor was enmeshed in those golden coils and poisoned his nephew, the heir to Milan."

"The wretch!"

"The doomed youth had a proud and high-spirited wife, Isabella of Aragon, whom Beatrice hated with a deadly hatred, and who would fain have placed the sickly lad, her husband, on his throne with her own strong arms; she besought and besieged her father, the King of Naples till he threatened to punish the Moor."

"Poor creature!"

"The Moor however was safe so long as the lord of Florence, the young Medici, stood between them. Medici was a mere tool in the hand of his beautiful,

and high-spirited wife, Alfonsina Orsini, and she persuaded the fool to make a friend and ally of the Moor.
Then the Moor called in the foreigner."

"Miserable man!"

"Thus three women enslaved Italy. The fourth —
you — must free it!"

"Chancellor, I am the wife neither of an old man
nor of a boy, nor of a fool, nor of a man who is in
any way to be beguiled by a woman. And — and I
wish for no crown." But she blushed the deepest
crimson.

"Madam," replied the chancellor, "the crown
wishes for you. Take pity on your nation and speak
for it to Pescara. I do not say coax, ensnare, beguile
him! I do not ask your collusion, I require no assumption of a part; I leave you to go to him and only
say let us see which of us will be with him soonest. If
you are there first clasp his knees, speak out of the
fulness of your heart, and say to him: ' Pescara, I am
Italy, and I kneel at your feet; raise me and take me
to your heart!' "

Vittoria was moved; the chancellor himself had
tears in his eyes.

"Illustrious lady," he went on, "who am I that I
should dare to speak to you thus? I am not worthy
to kiss the hem of your garment. Ludovico il Moro,
my gracious liege, picked me out of the streets of

Milan and let me play about his feet like a little dog
to amuse him. So I got my education, and at his
court, and his service I saw the men and manners of
the time — the whole reckless and triumphant course
of this century. — Unhappy Moor! His evil star and
the French invader dragged him away to Loches
where he pined in prison for ten long years. He was
near his end when I saw him again, there; for at that
time, by the force of circumstances, I was in the
service of the French, and I longed to behold the face
of my first benefactor. When I saw I was shocked; I
could scarcely recognize him. He looked like a
ghost; captivity and misery had strangely refined his
features. It was not till he spoke that I felt familiar
with him. He smiled and said with his own incomparable subtlety: 'Is it you, Girolamo? It is kind of
you to come to see me. — I owe you no grudge for
having gone over to the service of my foe. Circumstances are irresistible, and if I know you at all you
will be my sons' faithful adherent and adviser when the
wheel of Fortune has made a complete turn. You are
a ripe diplomatist now, and show the teaching of no
bad school. Do you still remember how I used to
forbid you to correct yourself of your comical physiog-
nomy and queer gestures? and it gladdens me to see
that they have won you universal favour.'

   " So he jested with me for a while in his magnani-

mous way, but then he became earnest and said: " Do
you know, Girolamo, what my one thought is in my
leisure here?   Not my own fate, but Italy — always
Italy.   I lament as the greatest torment of my soul
that, tempted by my wife, I invited the aid of the alien
nation with whom the day of reckoning is at hand,
and which threatens to become a canker in your flesh.
And I consider how Italy is ever to be herself again.
There was Valentino, that Caesar Borgia, who tried to
cure her with unmixed evil; but, Girolamo, my son,
evil can only be administered in small doses and with
great caution or it results in death.   And now there is
Rovere, that Pope Julius, who rides out on a thunder
cloud to repel the foreigners, whom he has brought
into the country quite as much as I.   But the old man
is burning himself out; his mighty soul will soon flit
down to Hades and his successor will be some com-
mon-place high-priest, a man too weak to lay the
foundations of Italy, and yet strong enough to hinder
others in the work of redemption.

    " Girolamo, my best-beloved, I do not think that
my Italy is perishing, for she bears in herself the
elements of immortality; but I fain would spare her
the penitential fires of servitude.   Heed me, my son:
I can read between your two eyes that you are destined to play a part yet in the mad whirl of events
which will sweep across my Lombard land.   If one

day a power should rise up from those changeful
forms, and a personage from among those transient
shapes — neither a criminal nor a priest, but a captain,
who can chain Victory to iron heels — be he who he
may, so long as he is not an alien, be wholly his, body
and soul! Whatsoever cunning and lies are needed,
take them on yourself, for without them no dominion
can be founded. He must remain stainless!"

The chancellor had sprung to his feet. His enthusiasm had carried him far beyond the limits of truth
without his observing it, nor did Vittoria notice it in
her excitement.

"That chosen one," he went on, "has the fairest
and purest of women at his side! Italy will see virtue
incarnate at her head and will imitate it. Our relaxed
morality has been our ruin, the violated girdle of
virtue. Here is a victory to be won, greater than any
in the field of battle; here is a magic wand to be
wielded, more mighty than the commander's staff. I
see her before me — that Queen of virtue, that Priest-
ess guarding the sacred fire, that woman who will
uphold the dominion; and lo, Hosanna! All Italy
follows in her train, jubilant and gleeful!"

The chancellor seemed to be on the point of falling
in homage at Vittoria's feet, but he drew back and
murmured bashfully: "These were Ludovico's words
in his dungeon."

Vittoria looked down, for she felt that her eyes were full of gladness and as bright as two suns.

Morone added:

" I have fatigued you, noble lady; your eyes are weary. You have to be off early to-morrow and are heavy with sleep." And the wily chancellor vanished in the darkness which had meanwhile closed in on the Eternal City.

CHAPTER III.

PESCARA was sitting at a window from which he could look out over the towers of Novara and the misty, sultry plain to the snowy peaks of Monte Rosa, still bright in the morning sun; he was studying the sketch of the campaign which was to carry the imperial army to the gates of Milan. His mind was so much absorbed that he did not hear his servant's soft step, and only became aware of his presence when the man offered him his morning glass of lemonade. As he stirred the light refreshment with a spoon he remarked to his attendant: " I do not blame you, Battista, for having come into my room last night against my express orders. Sleeping in the next room you may have heard me breathe more heavily than

usual — a nightmare, some oppression — nothing worth
mentioning," and he took a sip from the glass.

Battista, a crafty Neapolitan, hid his terrors under
a solemn face. He lied and asseverated by the holy
Virgin that he thought he had heard himself called by
name; never would he have ventured to enter his
highness' room without his orders; in point of fact he
had rushed in unbidden and against his master's strict
prohibition, prompted by a genuine human impulse.
He had heard Pescara groaning fearfully and had
raised him from his couch and supported him in his
arms till the marchese had recovered himself.

"It was nothing," Pescara repeated, "I needed no
help. But, as I said, I will not scold you now when
we are about to part. I am sorry to lose you; but
your filial duty must be done first, and as your infirm
old parents are living in misery at Tricarico I cannot
keep you from them. Go and make their last years
easy. You will always get on as a perfect barber and
a fluent rascal. — God be with you, my son; you
shall have no cause to complain of me," and he took
up a pen.

Battista was utterly astounded. He swore in his
despair, and with perfect truth this time, that his father
had long since gone to a better world, and that his
mother la Carambaccia, was well-to-do, in good
health, and as fat as an eel. The general, while he

wrote, merely replied: " To be sure; your parents are at Potenza and not at Tricarico; but they are not far apart." And he handed an order on his treasurer to the man he was dismissing.

Amazed and confounded as he was — for he knew that Pescara's lightest word was final — he càst a side-long glance as quick as lightning at the sum on the paper, most likely but a small one for his master was never a spendthrift in anything great or small, neither with his own money or the emperor's. Cursing the day when he was born in his bitter disappointment, Battista fell at his master's feet, clasped his knees and kissed his hand. " Farewell," said the marchese, " and clear that away." He pointed to the glass, and waved the man who had disobeyed him out of his service with a kindly gesture of dismissal.

But before he had again lost himself in his schemes he heard outside the clatter of a falling spoon and a broken glass, and the Duke of Bourbon roughly push-ing Battista aside, appeared unannounced, a tall figure in the doorway; for he had free leave to enter at any hour.

" Your highness ?" said Pescara, turning to him and rising.

" Pardon me; I was in the act of riding to join my troops when, as I was passing through the suburb, my eye fell on a travelling merchant getting off his mule at the door of your excellency's physician, Messer Numa Dati. But that this person had a dignified face, I could have sworn that it was my unforgetable friend the Chancellor of Milan. I sent one of my people to make enquiries and learnt that the traveller was a friend and guest of the leech's, a jeweller from Milan named Scipione Osnago. Perhaps so — or perhaps not; — perhaps only one of the many disguises assumed by the versatile Morone. He wriggled his person in a way not easily mistaken; so, as I had not yet passed out of the gates, I rode back to warn you of a possible visit from that delightful man."

" I have long been expecting him, with excuses and asseverations from his sovereign," replied Pescara, "but as he did not appear, and as we knew on good authority that his duke still goes on fortifying the town and arming his men, I began to despair of seeing the chancellor. Now he is too late. At midnight tomorrow, the term allowed to the duke will lapse. As twelve strikes out we march; unless, indeed, Morone brings some great news."

" Yes, indeed, this Morone! He will have concocted something by this time. When I pronounced our ultimatum at Milan I saw that there was a ferment in his brain like the scurry in an ant-hill. You can have no conception, Marchese, of his audacity. While I was governor of Milan, and he was my privy coun-

cillor and secretary, he used to dine with me, for I
enjoyed amusing myself with his stories and fancies;
and he would set me on every throne in turn and
marry me to every princess. And the maddest thing
was that there was reason in his folly. I am really
curious to know what he has been hatching now to get
himself and his duke out of the mess. It is sure to be
something infinitely ingenious — a mountain-top or an
abyss. Supposing, for instance," and the duke laughed
heartily, " he offered us — two imperial generals — the
leadership of the league, and as earnest-money pro-
duced two tempting Italian crowns from among the
folds of his toga."

" Your highness is jesting !"

" Not at all !" replied the duke preparing to go.
He grasped the marchese's hand and said in a gentle
tone which revealed a friendship unconfessed before
the world : " Pescara, I thank you for having kept
Leyva from my throat, by giving me the right wing
and him the left. I cannot ride side by side with that
intolerable man. Mischief would come of it, worse
than happened the other day in the market-place of
Novara. He might forget himself again in speaking
to me, and I could not help knocking him down like a
mad dog." He spoke in a low voice, with downcast eyes.

Pescara held the duke's hand and answered in
earnest warning :

"Such an outbreak!" he said, "and here, in the public market, about such a trifle as a choice of quarters! I sent Leyva at once to Naples to ask the viceroy for troops to join our campaign, though I knew he had none to give, merely to spare you embarrassment and the sight of a face you hate. — How could you behave so to your colleague. It was not well. It was most lamentable. It must not occur again — I beg, I entreat."

"The cause was unworthy, Pescara, but. . . ."

"The worst word that Leyva made use of as witnesses tell me was that he would take no orders from a prince, and you drew your sword, and your people had to hold you back."

"Indeed!" murmured the duke. "From a prince? — I have sharp ears, and it was another word, which I would thrust down the throat of the emperor or the pope. . . ."

"Another word?" said Pescara, but he regretted the question as soon as he had spoken, for the duke turned pale and bloodless. He guessed that the words used by old Leyva were that he would take no orders from a traitor, or that Bourbon's uneasy conscience had understood it so.

The unboastful friendship which subsisted between the unassuming nobleman and this scion of royalty, and which could work such a miracle as the stifling of

all natural jealousy between two young and already
famous captains, whose powers and relative position
were not too clearly limited, was based on the duke's
knowledge that his alliance with the foes of France did
not diminish Pescara's respect for him. Whether it
was prudence, or indifference to conventionalities,
or his freedom from even well-founded prejudice, or
the lofty justice derived from a consummate knowledge of men — Pescara had received the royal deserter
to the emperor's service with open arms, and behaved
to him with a subtle mixture of good fellowship and
courtly respect. Perhaps, too, he had discerned a
native and incorruptible nobility in this perplexed soul,
who cursed himself while he devastated his native land
with its enemies' weapons. And for this the duke was
grateful to Pescara.

The general, holding the hapless youth's hand,
spoke to him in a softened voice : " Mere fancy !
Your highness heard words that were not spoken.
Cast it from you. Strew the abyss with laurels ! Are
you not the favourite of the war god ? And a master
of state-craft ? Are we not both still young, with
many a day before us on this side of middle-life —
hardly half-way between twenty and thirty and in the
first third of a century overflowing with great possibilities and vast prospects. The fulness of life is ours !
Charles, let us live !"

Bourbon did not catch the suppressed sigh which escaped the warrior's breast. He warmly pressed Pescara's hand and his dark eyes flashed with a triumphant gleam. Then, to conceal his excitement, he leaped as it were head foremost into cynicism. It was a way he had, and Pescara's ardent tone had stirred his bold young blood.

"And we are both fine fellows," he exclaimed. "You, as the husband of the matchless Vittoria can understand that my heart and stomach rebelled when that *porcaccia*, the queen mother set her mind on having me for a husband at any price! Do you fancy me as father * of the King of France? A sweet, pretty stepson! — 'Madam,' said I, with a low bow, 'It would never do. Your nose would push me out of bed!' So right about face, and over the frontier!"

While he was still shouting with laughter, del Guasto came in covered with the dust of the journey; he greeted his uncle and bowed to the hilarious prince.

Then he addressed himself to Pescara — on whom he gazed with amazed and admiring eyes, as though the part he was intended to play in the Italian conspiracy had added to his stature — and began his story: "We set out from Rome with a numerous party, not to the marchesa's satisfaction; with Leyva,

* Francis I. His mother was Louise de Savoie, Duchesse d'Angoulême.

who has come back from Naples, and with a nobleman, of royal birth they say, who calls himself Moncada and whom you will know later. He is the bearer
of a message to you from the viceroy. I rode ahead
to announce Donna Vittoria's approach. She is full of
joy at the thought of seeing you again, but she keeps
her lips shut, for she has a political secret for your ear,
as I suspect — a papal mystery, I fancy; moreover,
Donna Vittoria frowns wrathfully at your nephew and
humble servant who has fallen into disgrace with her
and whom she means to indict with all formality
before you. About a question of humanity," and he
smiled.

" Or inhumanity," retorted Pescara. " And have
you any news, Don Juan ?"

" Unless my eyes deceive me the Chancellor of
Milan is in this town."

" Ah ha !" laughed Bourbon.

" I met him before in Rome, not far from the
Colonna palace, whither I was returning after dark. I
saw some one like a thief steal along under the wall in
a long robe, and when I threw a light on him from my
servant's torch, it was that snub-nosed, insolent fellow
with his crisp curls under a lawyer's beretta. I remembered him from Pavia, where he came to congratulate you after the fight. He may have been
there to bring some last private word from the pope to

Donna Vittoria, for she had taken leave of his Holiness that afternoon." This he said a little spitefully.

Pescara looked severely at him.

" Don Juan," he said, " you need not trouble yourself about Donna Vittoria's proceedings, and still less keep watch over them, I approve and applaud every step she takes, her lightest look or gesture."

Don Juan bowed.

" On my way to Novara," he went on, " I met Morone several times : that is to say, I came across a certain Paciandi, a fruit-seller from the Marches, with a dingy mole on his nose, who, when I questioned him, did not disguise the fact that he was very well-informed : an unexpected edict of the pope forbade exports and he had an important transaction to complete with your highness. And as he spoke he wriggled and made faces as like the chancellor as may be. Morone has all sorts of business on hand and cuts the strangest antics. He is to be seen here, there and everywhere, all over Italy, just like — but without any personal comparison — just like your own tall figure."

" What do you mean by that, Don Juan ?"

Del Guasto, though afraid of nothing, hesitated before Pescara's cold manner, and the duke's presence also checked him.

" I have no secrets from his highness," said the general. " Speak, Don Juan." But in spite of this command the common rumour seemed, even to the audacious youngster, too monstrous to repeat in this place and at this moment — in the heart of the imperial camp, and where through the open window he could hear the measured tread of the Spanish host marching past ; he was fain to throw a light veil over the shameless publicity of the Italian conspiracy.

"Uncle," he said lightly, "the rumour that still rings loudest in my ears is that of a furious discussion which has broken out among all ranks of men, in the taverns and barbers' shops, the fields where they play ball and, I firmly believe, even in the whispering corners of the sacristies, as to the real and legitimate nationality of the Avalos family — whether we are Neapolitans or Spaniards. And it is not confined to talk and gesticulation ; documents and letters are flying about, full of our birth and origin."

The general shrugged his shoulders. "My table was strewn with the rubbish," he said. "I have thrown it all away. Idle squabbling."

Don Juan turned perverse.

"I heard at the same time that there was a violent dispute going on at the universities, between the lawyers and theologians, as to the extent and limitations of the pope's rights as suzerain over Naples."

"That may be left to the doctors to settle. Do not you say so, your highness ?" said Pescara jestingly.

"And so far as the nationality of the Avalos is con-
cerned, nephew, I advise you to uphold their honour
whether Spanish or Neapolitan."

At this moment a page in waiting, a young boy
with large innocent eyes — a grandson of Numa Dati
and brother of that Giulia whom del Guasto had
betrayed — came in to announce an apothecary named
Baldassare Bosi of Orvieto, who was waiting with a
letter, in the ante-room, and would on no account be
denied. He had arrived, the lad said, at his grandfather's house, and Dati had given him a note to his
excellency. The boy handed Pescara the paper on
which was written in a trembling hand the name
" Morone."

The general thought for a moment. " Does the
stranger know that these gentlemen are here?" he
asked the page.

" I think not," said the boy.

" Then show him in; but mark, not till I call you."

He hastily turned to address the duke: " Your
highness must do me a favor. Since it is thought
possible that the Chancellor of Milan and I may be
conspirators together I should lack the commonest
prudence if I allowed the man who is waiting outside
to speak to me without a witness. I must have two
witnesses, and both trustworthy, to testify if not to our
identity, at any rate to every word we utter; so that

neither the suspicions of Madrid, nor Leyva's jealousy
nor. . . ." and he lowered his voice, " nor the villain
with whom you rode here, Don Juan, and who is here
to play the spy on me under the pretext of a message
from the viceroy — shall have any foundation for ac-
cusing me — I will not say of treason, but of a single
false step. Still, I must hear what the chancellor has
to say to me; in his folly and passion he will divulge
all the enemy's schemes and means. He can do it as
none other can. — Under the pressure of circumstances I pray your highness to condescend to play the
listener. And you, del Guasto, must keep his highness
company." He went to a heavy red curtain with gold
tassels whose broad folds, hanging to the ground,
screened the opening into the next room. He pulled
it aside: " Here, your highness will be quite hidden,"
he said.

Much as the duke was tempted by the stimulating
adventure he hesitated for a moment.

" Supposing Morone were to lift the curtain ?" he
said; and Pescara replied: " He will not. Do not be
afraid. I will answer for it." ·

Del Guasto's nostrils expanded with enjoyment;
he placed a seat for the duke and stood close behind
him as the second witness. The red curtain fell in
front of them.

Pescara found himself tightly embraced by Ippo-

lito, his page, who looked up at him whispering with
tears in his eyes : " He is no longer an apothecary, but
a magician in long black robes, with a talisman on his
breast and a terrible face !"

" You little coward !   Bring him in."

" Here he is !" cried Ippolito, and he fled.

" You, Morone ? And in your robes ?   But heated
by your journey, I see.   You must have found it hard
to breathe under three disguises."

Morone was gasping audibly for breath.   Drops of
sweat stood on his brow.   He stood speechless.

" What   is   your   worship's   errand ?"   asked   the
general with a grave look, but the chancellor could
not stammer out an articulate reply.   After a short
pause Pescara lightly laid his hand on the medal
which hung from a heavy gold chain round the chancellor's neck.

" A   Leonardo ?"   he   said.   " Whose   portrait ? —
The Moor's ?   A finely modelled head."   But Morone
could not take up the subject even of his beloved
master, so completely had he lost his self-possession.
Pescara therefore broke the ice without further ceremony.

" Your   duke,   Morone,   desires   more   favourable
terms ?   That may be open to discussion when his
highness shall have given me proof of his good intentions.   Let us go through my ultimatum point by

point." He went to the table and began to search for a paper.

He felt a hot breath on his cheek and a whisper poured into his ear. "Pescara," it gasped, "that is not what I have come for. Italy lays her army at your feet."

"That is well," replied the general without looking round. "It submits, then, to the emperor?"

But the voice at his ear cried out:

"Not to the emperor, but to you if you will desert him."

Pescara turned on the rash man with a gesture of hostile menace:

"You are mad! I do not know what should hinder me from seizing you and throwing you out of that window."

But Morone did not flinch; he stood firm, and cried again with flaming eyes: "This hour gives you your greatest chance, Pescara! Do not let it slip. You will rue it — you will die of it!"

"Hush! How loud you speak. If any one were listening — behind that curtain! — If I myself had . . . Do you think me incapable of such a trick? — Lift the hanging and convince yourself."

Morone had completely recovered himself when he had got over the shame and alarm of the first meeting. "Pescara," he said, "I have always found that the most cunning and most suspicious at last find them-

selves at a pass or in a cleft where they are compelled
to trust and to believe.   Thus it was with Valentino
and Rovere, with my beloved duke, the Moor, and his
captains and the Swiss. . . ."

"And both were betrayed, Morone!"

"Yes, Pescara.   But both the cunning Moor and
the remorseless Borgia perished trusting, and that cast
a bright gleam of humanity over the gloom of their
well-deserved overthrow.   At this moment, when I am
scheming a master stroke and require one of you,
would it not be childish to peep behind a curtain, like
a suspicious husband seeking for his wife's paramour?
— No, I give myself up! — Listen to me and then
hand me over to the executioner if you will."

"This is magnanimous," said Pescara without
irony, and then he added doubtfully: "Listen to you?
— My curiosity is excited, I confess, and I cannot
show the door to so heroic a man.   Still, tell me first,
Chancellor: Have I ever given you or your sovereign
any cause — even the smallest — to suspect my honour
as a commander?"

The chancellor said: "Never."

"Many lies are told: That his majesty has re-
warded me ill, and that I have taken it amiss. — If
you take your stand on the emperor's ingratitude, and
Pescara's dissatisfaction, I can but say, go not a step
further; you will sink in a quicksand!"

6

" I do not."

" Or are you emboldened by the common talk of
Italy which alternately flatters and suspects me, be-
lauds me and vilifies me ?   This Italian view of things
is a base machination.   It is intended to uproot me at
Madrid and to cripple me in Italy.   I have antici-
pated it and handed over to the emperor all the treacherous documents like vipers shut up in a cage. —
Did you dip a finger in that poison, Morone ?"

The chancellor turned pale.   " By all the gods of
Hades," he exclaimed, " I am guiltless of this !"

" Then you do not want to dupe me, Chancellor,
but to persuade me."

" Neither."

" What then ?"

" To convince you."

" That were best ; but it will take time.   Be
seated."   He hastily placed two chairs and they sat
down facing each other, Morone leaning forward over
his knees while Pescara leaned back in an easy attitude.

" Pescara, which was your greatest battle ; a marvel of military skill ?"

The general made no answer for none was needed,
but he sighed lightly.

" And what did the emperor make of the victory at
Pavia ?"   A lightning flash shot from Pescara's dark
grey eye.

" He flung it away," he muttered.

" You gave Charles a captive king, and he did not know what to do with him. He squeezed him like a money-lender. He demanded too much, and the impossible, instead of enough and the possible. ' Give up Italy, brother, that is your natural ransom, and you can yield it without injuring France. Give it up and depart.' — That is what a great conqueror would have said to King Francis."

Pescara smiled. " You are a dangerous man, Morone, when you guess at thoughts. But it is not I, it is you who give them utterance. I have said nothing."

" I thank the emperor," Morone went on lashing himself to excitement. " He aggrieved the goddess of victory after Pavia, and she is returning to you, my Pescara. Not only has she deserted the emperor; she is fighting against him. She has united all Italy to resist foreign rule, and she points to the leader. — Ah, my Pescara, what a conjunction of the planets protects and guides you! The hour is ripe and so are you! It is a fateful time, a desperate struggle — Gods and Titans, freedom rebelling against despotism — to-day the world is still moving and fluid, to-morrow it may be rigid as lava! The deed lies ready and waiting for you, and you were born to do it! Does not your hand long to be doing? It is a task for the intellect — laying an eternal foundation. — Look at the map and glance over the peninsula lying between two strips of sea and the mountain snows. Question history: it is a living body, often violently rent and always growing together again, a web of republics and principalities, with two ancient foes, two false ideas, two hideous chimeras: the pope and the emperor! Behold the outstretched finger of God! A new humanity is rising up: a humanity which can govern and ennoble itself without any supreme head, whether temporal or spiritual — a dance of freely developed genii, a concert of equally balanced states. . . ."

Pescara seized the soaring orator by the arm as if to hold him down: " Do not fly away, Girolamo!" he said laughing.

Morone shook him off.

" Let nothing hinder you in this divine work," he cried, " superstitious prejudice and antiquated ideas which have no place in your heart or your brain, or in the nature of things. I know you well, Pescara; you are a true son of Italy, and, like her, superior to pledges and conscience."

" Then you are an abominable race, you Italians," said Pescara, smiling. " But you make yourselves out greater villains than you are; for all this wisdom is not your own but borrowed from your familiar demon, the Florentine, who has crammed you with it. Is he still living ?"

The chancellor knew to whom Pescara referred. " He is·dying forgotten and contemned," he said with shame. " Our greatest thinker !"

" And he deserves it. There are some political maxims which have a real value for cool heads and cautious hands, but which are ruinous and reprobate when uttered by reckless lips or written with a corrupt pen. But that is true of all general rules ; everything depends on their application. For instance, Chancellor, what is your idea of the manner of my secession ?"

Morone opened his mouth as though his flow of speech would be inexhaustible; but Pescara lightly touched him with a finger :

" Gently, be cautious," he said. " You are treading on a very narrow and unsteady plank : it might happen that I should be compelled to put you in fetters as a conspirator at the end of your speech. Do not speak in your own person, I warn you ; but assume a mask, as you are so fond of doing — and why not that of the long-vanished Florentine secretary, whether he is still among the living or wandering among the shades ? — Speak, Niccolo Machiavelli. I will listen to you in silent admiration, and yet perhaps I may prove to you that you have too much imagination for a statesman. Oh ! I will criticize you, my worthy Niccolo. — But begin." The general's persistently ironical tone offended Morone; he was growing angry :

"Have done with jesting!" he exclaimed. "Do not degrade the man who risks his life to deliver his country to the level of a comedian! Pescara, I entreat you, be serious."

"Be serious? So be it," replied the general, shutting his eyes as though to listen better. The pale severity of the thin features gave Morone pause for a moment. But he was resolved.

"There is no harm done, Excellency," he began, "if you have given the emperor warning; it is well that you shonld remain in favour with him as long as possible, and only declare yourself when the pope and the league have put forth their manifesto. Meanwhile, strengthen your position and weed out your army."

Pescara raised his brows.

"Leyva must be got rid of," Morone went on.

Pescara began counting on his fingers.

"What are you calculating?" asked the chancellor, surprised.

Pescara calmly answered: "If Leyva must be got rid of my German officers must not be allowed to live, for they will be true to the emperor and his rule. Their heads must fall. — Or shall I pledge them in a poisoned cup? Which do you advise, Chancellor?"

Morone turned pale.

"And then what am I to do with my Spanish nobles? Must they, too, be murdered?"

"The Castilians," replied Morone with a fluttering heart will, no doubt, cling to their allegiance to the emperor. The rest you can tempt with endless booty; and they will not resist, least of all the Aragonese of Naples. I know the whole race; they are just like the pirate heroes of the New World. Only think of your del Guasto, — what a monster!"

Pescara did not contradict him.

"Your rank and file, which are gathered from all the lands on earth, you will impress by your unshaken strength of mind and your iron discipline, not to mention such regular pay as the emperor could never give them, while you command all the treasure of Italy. And if you suffer from the defection of your troops you can fill your ranks with Swiss who are to be had everywhere for hire since they threw away the position they had won and their foreign policy as well, for lack of guidance and of a national idea."

"A great pity," said Pescara to himself. He had a sort of tenderness towards this brave people, whom he had twice beaten, and of whom he destroyed at least a thousand at Bicocca in a few minutes by a particular disposition of his cannon which he had devised expressly to meet their furious onslaught. He loved them, though he owed his wound at Pavia to the thrust of a Swiss spear. "Their strength will not fail, but it is a pity," he repeated.

"Once sure of your army," Morone went on.

"I seize Milan," Pescara put in. "My plan is laid."

"You need not seize it, for the duke is a member of the league whose general you are."

"Very true; I had forgotten that. In any case Milan is the centre of action. And then?"

"You will find yourself in command of the armies of the Church, of Venice, and of Naples, not to mention the minor states."

"Stop, Morone. Naples is Spanish."

"By that time you will have sent your nephew thither as your viceroy; he will subdue it for you in a few weeks by his cruelties."

"As my viceroy? How long have I worn the crown of Naples?"

"The winged feet that bear it to you are already on the threshold," said the chancellor, reddening.

Pescara's cold expression brightened as if irradiated by a beam not from a crown but from the halo that shone round his coming wife.

"Another of your dreams, Morone," he said.

"Once at the head of the united armies of Italy and secure in your position," the chancellor went on with amazing assurance, "there is nothing to prevent your breaking with the emperor, perhaps even without a fight; for I know that you, though — nay, because — you are the greatest captain of the time prefer election to the chess-board tactics and absorbing calculations of strategy and the rough and always purblind decision of the battlefield. Perhaps, I say, without bloodshed; for the emperor will not easily find another general to collect another army in Italy when he has lost you and yours, at any rate if France and England give him work to do in consequence of their participation in our league."

"I am aware of your alliance with King Francis," Pescara said, "and the tenor of his word. But I do not count upon him. The king is fretting in his Spanish prison. If he is the man I take him for he would betray your league a hundred times over if it would set him free to leap into the saddle an hour sooner."

"Only a few days ago," said Morone with a comical grimace, "the Regent Louise wrote to me from Paris that she held the alliance as dear as her virtue. . . ."

A shrill "whew" was heard — the chancellor listened in amazement. A bird might have whizzed past the window.

"But there are others with whom the emperor has to deal," he went on. "The Crescent, and the German sovereigns."

"The Crescent, yes," the general said decisively.
"As to the German princes, the emperor might make
terms with them, and even with their new doctrines.
Do not you think so, Morone?"

Morone replied thoughtfully: "It seems so; but it
is not so if I see clearly. At any rate not as regards
the new creed. The emperor must have the Church
to comfort the gloomy and heavy temperament which
he inherits from his mother. The new creed appeals
to stronger souls."

"Have you any knowledge of these matters?"
asked Pescara with some interest.

"How should I, Pescara? I, like you and all of
us, am a son of Hellas, and live in the present. I
follow the wisdom of the ancients and see nothing
beyond the end but spectres and shades, and the
gigantic reflection of our own earthly life mirrored on
swaying mist. — Now, as you know, those who, like
the common people, believe in good and evil, and
body and soul, and the fable of the last judgment, are
fighting to the death as to the best way of preparing
for the call of that trump. Our Church very wisely
opens shop, and is ready to sell her stock of good
works. But the German monk rebels, and cries:
That is robbery. Do not waste your money. You
can have it all for nothing. Your debts are paid.
Only believe that and they are wiped out! But it

requires great courage to believe this, for of all incredible things it is the most incredible. Still, if these
German brains can do so they no longer need any
priests, and so have a great advantage in their arrogant confidence over us Italians, 'whether infidels or
superstitious. — I speak roughly; but these ideas,
though unimportant in themselves, are practically the
most real powers in life — powers which no statesman
may neglect with impunity; least of all you, Pescara,
with so great a task before you, even though you are,
as far as I know you, without a God."

But his smile met no response.

"In that you are mistaken," said Pescara gravely.
"I believe in a God and verily in no unreal one. —
For the rest, you are right; I have seen it with my
own eyes. On the evening after my battle — " he
meant that of Pavia — "I saw in the hospital two men
die, both guilty wretches, a German and a Spaniard.
The Spaniard lay trembling and quailing in the arms
of two priests, clutching a reliquary; the other was
dying alone but full of assurance and joy. I spoke to
him, knowing a few words of German, and he told me
he trusted confidently in mercy to the repentant
sinner. — But, enough of these shades of faith. Let
us return to the matter in hand; for I suppose you
have not said all you have to say."

"By no means. — As soon as you have got the

emperor out of the game by the sword or by some compromise, you may begin to build up your own greatness and the freedom of Italy. The twelve labours of Hercules! — But every quality and characteristic of your mind will rise in arms: Patience and decision, enthusiasm and calculation, craft and magnanimity. Not a fibre of your nature must lie idle. You do not yet know yourself, Pescara. Not till then will you show the man you are, at your full stature; to the people a terrible but beneficent demon; to the army an infallibly victorious captain; to patriots the redeemer of Italy; to the learned a resuscitation of old Roman ambition; to the princes — such as you allow to remain, — a leader and ally. All the possibilities and favouring circumstances of the age are at your command. You will become the pope's chief champion and reconquer for him the towns and provinces he has lost — to keep them for your own; you will ride forth as arbitrator in Florence between the republic *in extremis* and the Medici, and both will obey you. Even the Queen of the Adriatic will be drawn within the magic circle of your power, and I can see you made Doge and wedding the sea! — Thus you will grow in greatness till you and your beautiful wife are hailed at the capitol, till a thousand welcoming hands lift you up to be worshipped and show you to Italy as her King. Then, when she is your possession

and your pride, you will, I hope, love her a little —
though you do not now — and thus end where I
begin; for it is my devotion to Italy — the best, the
only good thing in me — which has brought me to
your feet, cold-hearted man that you are!"

He threw his arms round Pescara's knees with such
fervent devotion that the general started to his feet to
draw away from such adoration; still, he seemed
deeply stirred, whether it was that such genuine feeling
from so false a spirit captivated him, or that his powerful intellect involuntarily completed a vivid image of
the greatness of Italy and of his own prospects thus
briefly outlined.

He turned away and paced the room several times,
his arms folded over his breast; at last he paused in
front of the chancellor, as if by accident.

"How many years of my life do you ask of me,
Morone?" he said.

"Many, no doubt, very many," replied the chancellor. "The more the better. But broken by those
long and fruitful pauses in which things grow silently
and vigorously, gnawing through obstacles that looked
insurmountable, dulling and quieting men's consciences,
and even expiating and sanctifying the initial crime;
for it is only by such slow, broad stages that anything
permanent can be accomplished in a State. Life,
Pescara, is your best ally. Ten, twenty, why not

thirty years? You are in the fulness of strength and have as yet but dipped your hand into the brimming fount. You have scarcely laid a hand on your store, and not the least of the reasons why the undying gods of Italy have called you of all men to this glorious task, is because you are still young, as Romans count, and no shadow of Death can fall on you for a long time to come."

Suddenly a harder and more ominous expression had darkened the great captain's face. He cast such a fierce eye on Morone as made him shrink back a step.

"And do you not know," he thundered, "that if I allowed my ambition to get the upper hand, your master, Sforza, would be the first victim? For I should begin by giving your Milanese to the Duke of Bourbon, who is my *alter ego*, my right hand, and a Gonzaga. I would bestow it on him. Are you prepared to deliver Sforza into my hands?"

"By all the gods, no!" cried the horrified chancellor. "I, betray the duke? Never, never! Besides," he went on wrathfully, "how dare you, Pescara, think of staining our great and sacred cause with a Bourbon?"

"What a man!" said Pescara with bitter scorn. "Can anything be more audacious? He will keep his faith to his miserable princeling but tries to persuade

me to break mine to my glorious emperor! What an
illogical, inconsequent mind! I am to be incited to
treason, but he is to keep clear of it!"

"That is quite a different thing," said the chancellor. "The Connétable de Bourbon has betrayed
his country; now you would save yours by deserting
from a sovereign who is not your master. — I, sacrifice my duke, my beloved young lord? The Moor
will haunt me in my dreams!" he sighed piteously —
"And yet, well — so be it! But now, Pescara, you
can resist no longer. Have mercy on Italy? Answer,
cruel man!" and tears started to his eyes.

"Not to-day, Morone," said Pescara soothingly.
"We are both tired and need rest. It is the hour of
siesta." He rang a bell. "Ippolito," he said to the
page, "conduct my lord, who is a great statesman, to
the turret-wing. The major-domo is to throw open all
the rooms on the top-story, and wait on him punc-
tually, and entertain him worthily. You will find a
well-chosen library, Chancellor, and if you wish to take
the air pray go down into the garden; it is shady and
extends as far as the city walls. I do not invite you
to dine with me as I am expecting Donna Vittoria,
and my evening belongs to her. Do not let time hang
heavy on your hands. To-morrow we shall meet again."

"How shall I get through the day?" said Morone
lamentably.

"Everything comes to an end. One thing more :
Let me beg of you not to go near the men on guard.
You do not understand German."   He saw the chancellor turn pale. "You have nothing to fear," he
added kindly, and Morone left the room.

As he turned round, the duke and del Guasto, who
had quitted their lurking-place, came towards him,
both in the greatest excitement ; Bourbon, usually so
pale, with crimson cheeks ; del Guasto with a fire in
his eyes. Pescara divined that the conversation they
had overheard, with its suggestions of glory, had bewitched and deluded them. Del Guasto was hunger-
ing for plunder, and the duke for laurels to reinstate
him. They said nothing, but their eager and implor-
ing looks were on the point of finding expression when
Pescara stopped their mouths.

"Well, my lords," he said, "we have had a dram-
atic performance. The piece was rather long ; did
you not yawn in your box ?"   Bourbon, with a quick
revulsion of feeling, burst into loud laughter. "Tragedy or farce ?" he asked.

"Tragedy, your Highness."

"And the name is. . . . ?"

"Death and the Fool," replied Pescara.

CHAPTER IV.

THE Chancellor of Milan wandered restlessly in and out of his extensive apartments. The shutters were closed to keep out the scorching mid-day sun; only here and there an intrusive ray peeped into the gloom through a chink, making a vivid streak on the stone floor, while the rest of the room remained in the mystery of darkness. Not the faintest gleam of light illuminated Morone's mind as to Pescara's. He had poured out his own heart to the very dregs; Pescara had revealed no tittle of his; and the chancellor was, at this moment, not merely guilty by his own confession, but also a prisoner, or little short of it. Still, far from repenting of having laid his soul bare, or from being uneasy at his captivity, he revelled, on the contrary, in a sense of magnanimous self-abandonment. Even the thought of the prince he had so basely betrayed did not now disturb his conscience, so entirely was he possessed by the passionate desire to over-master Pescara, and by the excitement of his attack on that remarkable man, whose lordly attitude and grave skill in their interview he sincerely admired. He continued the scene in fancy: every word of the dialogue still rang in his ears, he felt every look and

7

gesture repeating itself in his features and the very twitch of his limbs; but as to the meaning and purport of what had been said he entangled himself in inextricable and agonizing doubts. He rejected one theory after another, ending at last with the probable assumption that Pescara was as yet undecided, and still fighting the battle with himself.

Then he remembered with anxious longing the fair ally who might arrive now at any moment, and Vittoria Colonna's value in the cause seemed to him inestimable. Only such a woman as she could win over such a man. It was not one of the aspiring domineering women of whom there were so many then in Italy, but the noblest lady of her time who would plead his cause; and in her person, as the incarnation of Italy's every beauty and virtue with none of her weakness, his native land seemed so matchless, and the glory of serving it so unique, that even Pescara — nay, Pescara of all men — surely could not resist her. The League, even though its instruments were base, was transfigured by those heavenly eyes, to such purity as justified its name of the Holy League in a broad and worldly sense. His admiration of the divine creature who, as he believed, was destined to save Italy, rose to adoration and fervent rapture, for he was capable alike of the loftiest and the basest feelings in equal degree and violence.

As the confidence he had thus gained threw a light
on his mind he pined for daylight; he pushed open a
shutter and stood looking about him. He was in
the serpent-room, as it was called, of which he had
often heard his duke speak but which he had never
before seen. All round it above the panelling, was
painted a twisted pattern of snakes, entwined two and
two : one, the fire-breathing dragon of the Sforza, the
other, the hideous badge of the Visconti — a serpent
with a child in his jaws. Whether it were a legend or
the truth, the gentle Leonardo da Vinci was said to
have devised this alarming frieze; in the course of his
long employment in the Moor's service he had once
passed a short time in the ducal palace at Novara,
where in a few hours, he had designed and finished
this sport of grim fancy under the pretext of doing
honour to his master's family. It was not impossible,
for the painter of mystical smiles was much addicted
to monstrosities and horrors.

The chancellor examined the intricate design, at
first with interest and then with tortured eyes following the various and natural contortions in which the
artist's dauntless imagination had depicted the dragons
and the naked child. Then suddenly he fancied the
knotted creatures were alive and writhing.

Turning away with a shudder he went to the window and looked down into the lonely castle-garden

which slumbered in the shadow of a dense arcade of trees. Above, there was nothing to be seen but a flood of dazzling light framed in here and there by the battlements of the city walls. At a little distance off a small villa was visible, rising from a perfect thicket of verdure. It stood at an angle on the uppermost of three terraces and he could see two sides of it, each of which had a character of its own. One ended in a little tower, the other had a vine-grown verandah. The various parts, different as they were in size and style formed a harmonious whole, and Morone could not help thinking that this pretty residence must be intended for Vittoria by her husband, who would give her a loving welcome, not in this gloomy castle, echoing with the tramp of men on guard, but in yonder peaceful and pleasant retreat. The bustle of servants about the villa pointed to the expectation of a guest, and he fancied indeed that he could hear the noise of an arrival from the opposite side. He could no longer endure the warm room; he found his way to a staircase and door, and presently was walking in a maze of green shade.

The path led to a large round arbour where delicious twilight reigned, while in the centre a spring filled its glittering basin with a sleepy, slowly-flowing, translucent tide. Four marble benches stood round it, and on one of these, with sculptured sphinxes for arms, Pescara was sleeping, his head bent over his breast.

After his first surprise, Morone stole forward with a cautious step to see if the sleeping face might not unconsciously reveal the unconfessed mind of the man. He stood there for some time. No; it betrayed no dreams of ambition, no schemes of treason; the uncontrolled features bore no trace of triumph or cunning; their expression suggested nothing but pain and self-sacrifice. As Morone gazed, his own mobile features grew rigid, for those of the motionless sleeper were so eloquent that a fatalist mood came over him, an irresistible conviction of the nothingness of human projects and the omnipotence of fate. The powerful face spoke only of resignation and submission.

A hand was laid on Morone's shoulder. He started with a sort of uncanny fear, as though the double of the sleeper before him had stolen behind him; then he turned round and saw a yellow, bald head, and a figure bent by age. Two shrewd brown eyes with an expression of intense sadness were the only living things in that face.

"Numa! It is you? You gave me a fright."

"I quite believe it. But come, Chancellor; we will leave him to sleep, and sit down yonder that I may watch him from a distance."

They did so, and the physician, who must have

been at least eighty years of age but had not lost his acute hearing, began a whispered conversation with Morone.

"You think you have won him over?" he asked.

"I do not know," said the chancellor. "*Est in votis.*"

"Do not deceive yourself, Girolamo! I tell you: even if he were willing he cannot."

"He cannot? Why not? That sounds most mysterious. What god or goddess forbids it? Do not torture me. Speak."

"If I might have spoken I would have warned you from crossing my threshold, and from Novara; but my lips are sealed. Still, poor wretch, I cannot let you rush on perdition. You are wasting your words here, perhaps risking your life. He cannot — I repeat it. It is denied him; it is not granted to him. — Fly! It is all in vain."

"Fly? From Pescara? I have no thought of such a thing. I have him fast! By all the demons, why is it not granted to him?"

The physician murmured, so softly that Morone could scarcely hear him, "Is not man's mortal course in time and space? And both are denied him?"

He laid his finger on his lips to enjoin silence, and then again he whispered to warn the chancellor of approaching footsteps: "Hush — look!"

Vittoria Colonna came lightly into the green bower,

seeking her husband in his favourite retreat. Her
dress still bore traces of the dust of the road; she must
but just have slipped from the saddle. Seeing that he
slept she stood still, absorbed in watching him. Then
she suddenly melted into tears, overcome by joy — or
perhaps touched by the solemnity of the face she
loved, graven as it was by toil and wounds. But in a
minute or two she went close up to him. She tenderly
laid her hand on the grand head and gently woke him
with a deep kiss. Pescara opened his eyes; he clasped
his wife in his right arm and kissed her brow.

As he rose, Morone, in an unwonted fit of bashful-
ness, slipped away, and Pescara saw only the physician. Putting the other arm round Vittoria's waist
he held out his hand to Numa, saying to his wife:
" This is my leech!" and she in her eager way knelt
and covered his thin hand with kisses. "You healed
my hero's wounds!" she exclaimed with glad gratitude; then rising, she asked with some agitation:
" You are Messer Numa Dati?"

The old man bowed.

And Vittoria, carried away by her warm heart,
turned to her husband, lip to lip, and said: " Before
we rejoice you must do justice to me and to this good
man. — Our nephew has betrayed his granddaughter,
and the wretch refused to atone for his crime by
marrying her."

"Is it so, Numa?" said the general; and when the old man sadly confirmed it he added: "And why did you conceal this from me?"

"In the first instance, my lord, it was merely a supposition, for she left my house and Novara secretly. And how could I dare to trouble you, who have your own great destiny to bear, with the trivial sorrows of a girl? Not till to-day, indeed, have I been made certain by a letter from Rome, from the abbess of the convent in which the poor child had taken refuge."

Vittoria imploringly clung to her hero, leaning against his left side; the pressure of her body seemed to cause him pain. To conceal and bear it he moved forward a few steps, and the three stood watching the play of light on the water.

"My sweet wife, how I have longed to see you once more!" said the soldier. "And now I have you here, my own soul." He looked into her beaming eyes. "But your eyelids are still heavy with the dust of the journey. Give me your handkerchief." She gave it him to dip in the fountain, and closed her eyes while he bathed her forehead and eyes and cheeks.

"I remember your granddaughter very well, Numa," he went on, "though I scarcely saw her. Dark blue eyes and chestnut hair like this, has she not? And Giulia is her name? Hers seems indeed a hard and tragical case. Not that I should hesitate to force the villain — for you know, Vittoria, I can call him nothing else — to marry the girl; he would obey me no doubt, for he is in my power and I can control his actions. But I cannot but ask myself whether it would be well to fetter her in her disgrace to a heartless and cruel man, though his daring and talents will carry him to the highest position. And she herself. — Will she ask it? Do you think so, Vittoria? Did she desire it when she threw herself — as I suppose — at your feet in Rome, — for you know her?"

"She did indeed," said Vittoria beseechingly.

"Could she bear your pure presence? — Then seriously you would give her to the man who despises her? If she were my child I would bury her in the cloister. But you are humane and compassionate, Madonna; and who knows, perhaps she loves him still, or loves and hates him both. — I do not understand such matters. But I will take the matter up; she shall have her choice."

The physician opened his sunken lips. "Poor Giulia!" he said. "And what a choice! Happy for her that she is above such an alternative!"

"How?" Pescara enquired.

"By the act of an inscrutable but wise Providence."

"I understand," said Pescara quickly, "she is no more."

" It is so, my lord."

" She laid hands on herself?" cried Vittoria. " May her guardian angel forfend !"

" Who knows ?   She died on her return to the convent, after making her confession to you. That confession must have killed her, and the sight of your pure face, Madonna, as my lord said. Perhaps her heart was broken, perhaps — the girl was handy, and had often given me intelligent and skilful help in my pharmacy."

" The general said : " It must remain unexplained. No one can see into such darkness. She is now standing in the presence and service of a sacred Power who mocks at our puny justice."

" Pescara !" cried Vittoria sadly, and the old man added :

" I can say no more !   It is well."

" Yes, it is well," replied the general.

He turned to Vittoria and holding out his hand said more lightly :

" Noble lady, I have fitted up for you and myself, so long as we may be together, a brighter home than this old castle with its ponderous beams — this lurking-place of treason, for it was on the castle draw-bridge that the Moor was betrayed. — Look, Madonna, do you see that pretty villa through the pines ? That is intended for you.   It suits your blameless life."

They walked through the park as far as the three flights of terrace steps; there the old physician stopped to take breath, and await the general's return. When Vittoria reached the third terrace she perceived two statues to the right and left of the top flight.

"That was young Francesco Sforza's idea," said Pescara. "His taste in such matters is always the best. These groups are the charming notions of his giddy brain. This to the right, for instance. At first I could not make out what it meant, much as I admired it. Then the gardener told me of an inscription it had originally borne, and which the ingenious young duke had had defaced, that the spectator might feel and guess the meaning. It was — but can you guess it, dear love?"

Vittoria, after glancing hastily at the group to the left, a pair clasped in a fond embrace, stood for some time contemplating the other. It consisted of two female figures, one lying down and idly plucking to pieces a flower or a butterfly; the other standing lost in thought or gazing at the distance. All three of the girlish figures however — kissing, thoughtless and meditative — had the same features with a different expression. Vittoria thought in vain. The general bent down and whispered in her ear like a boy prompting a girl at school: "Use your eyes; a few letters are still legible," and on the left hand statue she discerned though very faintly, the letters Pres. . . . . . and on the other, rather more plainly, Ass. . . . . . "Presenza" and "Assenza," she said and Pescara said: "*Presence* is confidently bold. Absence forgets and does not care. What I value is presence in absence: yearning."

"If you love me, Fernando, we will never part again."

"Only once more. For a few days — a week at most, Madonna — till I have taken Milan. Then you shall follow me; and thenceforth, if you wish it, we will never again separate. It rests with you, Vittoria," he said tenderly.

"If I wish it!"

"Do you remember, love," he went on lightly: "How once, in Ischia, by the plashing sea, you said that you could not understand how any woman who had once loved could ever marry a second time? It was contrary to the idea of love, you thought. And yet experience and human nature are against you. Absence, absence!"

Vittoria drew herself up — and she was nobly tall. She raised her beautiful arm to heaven, her sleeve falling back as she moved, and swore: "Never will I be another man's wife, by the pure light of that sun!"

Pescara spoke soothingly: "There are your waiting-women, child, wondering at your vow — nor are they minded to follow your example." He beckoned

to the maids who were lingering at a respectful distance and took leave of his wife.

" Now you will want to change your dress, and I
have much to do before evening.   Till we meet again,
here, after sundown, at supper."

He turned away and did not look back.   At the
bottom of the steps he took the old leech's arm and
slowly they made their way through a cypress avenue
leading to the castle.

" How did your Highness pass the night ?" asked
the physician.

" As usual," replied Pescara.   " You were strictly
discreet with your guest I hope, Numa ?"

" I bore your commands in mind. — But how
could you play so cruel a trick on the chancellor and
my hapless country !   How dared you ?"

" I play a trick on Italy, do you say ?   On the
contrary, your countrymen, Numa, are playing with
me : they pretend to be alive and they are dead in
their transgressions and sins."

They walked on in silence till presently Pescara
said ironically : " Do you know, Numa, an astrologer
came to see me not long since and cast my horoscope ?
He gave me sixty years of life. I thought that but little."

The old man sighed, and again they went on in
silence.   Pescara dismissed his companion at the narrow gate into the castle.

" My officers are waiting for me, I put them off till this hour."

Then a pang of compassion came over him as he looked at those kind brown eyes and that toothless mouth, and he said : " Fear nothing, Numa. I will do no harm to your Italy ; I will be just and lenient."

In his anteroom he found the Duke of Bourbon and Leyva face to face, with del Guasto between them, as though he were keeping them apart; and besides these a fourth person, leaning against the side of a window-bay : a distinguished-looking man of advanced age, half-monk, half-warrior, with a bronzed face and large hard features. He was wrapped in a white cloak resembling a friar's cowl. As Pescara saw him he seemed to shudder slightly, but he went up to him and greeted him :

" What procures me this honour, Moncada ?"

" Your Excellency," replied the other, " I come as an envoy, and desire an interview in the viceroy's name."

" I grant it," replied the general, " but I must beg your Grace to be brief; we are on the eve of a march."

" A secret interview."

Pescara reflected.

" Secret ! No, Cavaliere. I have no business secrets from these two gentlemen, my coadjutors. Spare me any discussion. My nephew is to be trusted.

— What is your message? Speak." But he did not offer Moncada a seat.

Moncada looked keenly at the faces round him: "As you will," he replied. "My lord, the viceroy, is in great anxiety. The Italian League is an accomplished fact. Of this your lordship can entertain no doubts, since you sent Leyva to ask the viceroy for troops. However, he cannot spare them, as he needs them himself to enable him, in the event of war, to make a respectful but hostile display of force against his Holiness who has joined it — either wilfully or under evil influence. Your Excellency will allow that our armies in the north and south of the peninsula must act in concert. To this end the viceroy sends me to attend you, and keep him informed of the progress of affairs. I have your consent?"

The general assented, swallowing down his vexation.

"Yet further," Moncada went on. "I can but regret that you would not grant me a private audience, but I must seize the opportunity. It is hoped that when your Excellency has seized Milan you will take severe and comprehensive measures there to secure the safety of the monarchy and strike at the root of the evil. You are therefore advised: that the duke is to be put in chains and sent to Spain: that the rebel nobles of Lombardy must forfeit their estates and mount the scaffold: that the citizens are to be subju-

gated by a strong garrison and a heavy war-tribute:
Terror is to reign in Milan!"

He tried to read the expression of Pescara's face.
The marchese stood calm.

"Terror!" he said.   " Never, so long as I live and
serve the emperor.   Milan is a fief of the empire and
the emperor will allow no portion of the empire to
suffer ill-usage. — Hoped !   Advised !   By whom ?
You may spare such hopes and advice, Moncada; I
do not need them."

"Has the duke begged for delay?" asked Moncada suspiciously.

" No, Cavaliere."

" Not through his chancellor ?"

" The chancellor of his highness of Milan has this
day come under my roof. Your Excellency can see
him and question him, — and so procure him a pleasure, for I fear he is but dull."

"And you have not seen him ?   I ask not out of
curiosity, but in the interests of the royal cause, which
all here present serve."

" I saw the chancellor this morning and spoke with
him for two hours."

This frankness amazed Moncada but it told him
nothing. He was fully informed of Morone's arrival
and interview with Pescara by the spies he subsidized
among the general's followers.

"A long interview. It can only have related to the duke's submission."

Pescara said nothing. A secret aversion, as it seemed, kept him from vouchsafing a single word more than was absolutely necessary to the man before him.

"I only wonder," Moncada went on, "that your Excellency did not cut it shorter, and it amazes me to think that you should have admitted that abject wretch at all now that Italy is ringing with calumnious rumours of your conduct."

"Say no more! Another word would be an insult — and loss of time. I have reported those lies to my emperor. That is enough. I know my enemies. . . ."

"Very wise. And it would have been equally wise if you had given Morone audience within hearing of trustworthy witnesses."

"I did so," said Pescara contemptuously. "These two gentlemen." Bourbon and del Guasto bowed. "As regards the matter of our discussion which you seem so curious to know, you may learn it in the answer I propose to give the chancellor to-morrow — in your presence, if you will — before he follows in my train as a prisoner. — Here, in this room. — For the present I leave you." And he withdrew into his own room followed by the other three.

Moncada remained alone. "A mask!" he muttered. "An elaborate mask! What face does it con-

8

ceal? I will see it. You shall not evade me, Pescara!" and he slowly quitted the castle, full of conflicting thoughts.

While the three captains within were planning war, the anteroom remained for some time unoccupied and unguarded. Ippolito had stolen away to his mistress's villa; he had seen her arrive and admired her beauty and condescension with boyish adoration. He was burning to pay her his duty and offer his services.

Presently the solemn room was filled with a riotous company. The Connétable de Bourbon's five silver greyhounds, frolicsome creatures, but just out of puppy-hood, had found their way into the castle and were now sniffing at the door behind which they knew that their master was sitting. These dogs were the fashion. Then the marchese's hunting-dog, a noble beast and an indefatigable courser, came to see what was going on and was much edified by the frivolous party which, in his opinion, had no business there, and to whom he expressed his disapproval by growling. Ere long another visitor appeared: a frail and delicate grey-hound, with a bright silver collar bearing the inscription: " I belong to Vittoria Colonna." Welcomed at first with delight and admiration the small dog was in a few minutes a hunted and frightened creature, with the whole puppy pack barking and yelping at his heels. Then the page came flying in, seized his mis-

tress's pet which he had been sent to fetch, and carried
it out of the skirmish, the whole pack following in
pursuit with the exception of Pescara's sober hound.
At this moment Leyva came out of the inner room
and hastened the general retreat by giving the last dog
a kick which sent it howling through the air.

The grey-headed soldier's face was red with rage
and he was hardly to be detained by Pescara's per-
suasive hand. "Leyva," said the marchese, "I entreat
you, stay. Control yourself! I cannot compel you to
be just to the duke, but at any rate behave with
decorum. The duke treats you with exemplary consideration, and perfect courtesy, while you make a face
at him like a snarling peasant; and you are running
away before our council is ended. Such conduct ill-
beseems your position and your merits."

"I could not endure the traitor any longer, Pescara. His every look, every movement revolts me
from the crown of my head to the tip of my toes. His
coolness is contempt, and his bows a mockery of mine.
Such consummately royal scorn! I should like to
know what right he has to make a parade of it! I am
his superior, in spite of his high birth, for my honour is
unstained and I am a faithful servant of my sovereign,
while he has deserted his. He is a marked man, and
his smooth face is fouler than my hideous scars!
However, I am not looked down upon by every high-

born noble; there are some who know my real worth.
— For instance, Moncada, who travelled with me: a
very sensible man.   He, at any rate, honoured me
with his confidence."

Pescara was very grave.

"Leyva," he said: "You will give me the satisfaction of admitting that I have always appreciated you.
I care for no accidental distinctions, least of all for
that of birth; but I take men as I find them.   Have
you ever seen me arrogant or found me unjust? —
You have no grievance with me, old friend," he said
warmly, "we know each other."   And his keen grey
eyes tried to meet those of his colleague who obstin-
ately held his head down and avoided his gaze.

"None," murmured Leyva, "excepting that you
keep up your friendship with that man.   But I am in
haste; your Excellency will send me your instructions.
I shall be glad to have them in writing.   Leyva will
do his duty; rely upon that."

The marchese allowed him to depart and thoughtfully stroked his dog who had pushed his head under
his master's hand.

Then he went back into the inner room where he
found Bourbon and del Guasto in eager discussion,
over something relating to the chancellor it would
seem, for they were looking in the direction of the
tower.   The general smiled.

"My lords," said he, "you overheard a strange discourse this morning, and — which is stranger still — that discourse did not delude me but you — my witnesses. My fidelity is untouched, and yours has been shaken I fancy: a triumph flattering to Morone and which he had not counted on."

Then turning to del Guasto he went on: "Don Juan, I saw the greedy sparkle in your eyes at the word plunder. You may thank me for not allowing you to speak, and so betray your emperor. For you, of all men, Don Juan, must keep spotless faith with his majesty unless you would be a criminal. Fidelity to your sovereign is the only virtue of which you are yet capable, and the last notion of honour that is left to you. It will help to redeem your inexorable nature if you exercise it against desertion and rebellion, and if your cruelty serves the cause of earthly justice. Take this as my well-meant advice. — Now go, and avoid Donna Vittoria's eye. She hates the sight of you: she cannot endure a murderer."

"A murderer?" Don Juan fired up.

"A murderer. — Do you not know who your victim is? — I will tell you. It is Giulia, my friend Numa Dati's granddaughter, who has died in Rome of a broken heart, and it was you who brought her to it. It is happy for her; but that does not in the smallest degree mitigate your guilt. Do not be afraid that she

will haunt you. She rests in peace leaving you to the
Furies of your soul, sooner or later to remorse."

Del Guasto turned pale; he felt as if his hair stood
on end like a tangle of snakes. His deed had less
terrors for him, indeed, than his captain's awful
severity; its annihilating condemnation was like a sentence from beyond the grave. He vanished abashed
from the lightnings of those eyes.

" Family affairs," Bourbon remarked. " But do
you know, Fernando, the chancellor stirred my enthusiasm more than you fancy? In spite of his insinua-
tions — he is the only man from whom I do not take
them ill — he was in a fair way to befool me; or
rather it was you, when you spoke of me as your *alter
ego*, and said you would give me Milan. You, in fact,
made game of me, and I, like an idiot, did not understand the joke."

" Forgive me, Charles! I wondered whether the
chancellor would be true to his own duke. But take
my word for it, for you, too, the imperial cause is the
only one. Italy must succumb; it is inevitable; the
country is undermining itself. Look fairly at the
situation : Italy offers herself to me, on her knees and
unconditionally, with a semblance of truth and magnanimity; and at the same time, with amazing cunning, she tries to cut the ground from under my feet,
to compel me to leap across the gulf. — I can quite

understand that hearing such rumours and calumnies
Madrid should send some one to watch me and play
eaves-dropper. But why, my enemy? Why, Moncada? It is true he can find no hold on me, and I
shall finish my day's work and give you, Charles, all I
have to give : my place and the results of my work. —
You will be just to Italy will you not, Charles? You
will not torture her nor oppress her beyond measure?
Promise me this! — Though she has not deserved so
well of me. — But you will be humane in your
dealings?"

" With all, excepting his Holiness who has vilified
me. — But what are you saying, Fernando? You
alarm me! We are of the same age, and a cannon-
ball may kill me before you — or both of us together.
This Moncada has fallen on you like a blight, I saw
you shudder. What is it that stands between you?"

The sun was now sinking; there was a soft rap at
the door. Ippolito came in and said humbly to his
master : " My lord, you will not keep madonna waiting. Supper is ready and madonna is on the terrace—
unless she has come down."

" Go, child, and say that I am coming."

" Nay, that I will not," replied Ippolito with play-
ful defiance, " for if I go your excellency will begin
some endless political discussion with his highness, and
forget the sweet lady."

The marchese liked to have the boy about him, but
in resuming the discussion with the duke, round whose
shoulders he had confidingly laid his arm, he spoke in
Spanish, of which language he knew that his page did
not understand a word.

"What stands between me and Moncada? A
hideous thing — a suspicion nay, a fact to me, but of
which I have no evidence but my own convicions.   I
believe — indeed I am sure that Moncada killed my
father."   He stroked the boy's hair, and the innocent
eyes looked up at his face.

"It was at the end of the last century, and I was
about the age of this child, certainly not older.   My
father, a good soldier and a better man than I, and a
trusting soul, went to Barcelona as envoy from the
viceroy at that time, the great Gonsalvo who afterwards had such cruel experience of Spanish ingratitude.   At that time old King Ferdinand held his court
at Barcelona.   My father there met the last scion of
our royal Neapolitan race: the unhappy youth who
was destined to fade under Ferdinand's suspicious eye,
leaving a childless wife. — Guileless and imprudent as
my father was — and a simpler soul never breathed —
he allowed himself to be betrayed into sympathetic
conversation with the dethroned prince and visited him
occasionally at the palace: this was enough to make
the king suspect him, and that suspicion led to his death.

"I tell you the tale as I subsequently pieced it out after patient enquiry, and as past events gained sense and meaning to my maturer comprehension and experience of mankind. It is highly probable that the king himself had designated the victim, if only by a half-hint or significant gesture, but he left the execution of his unspoken sentence to a young man who was always about his person, and who was said to be his natural son. Young Moncada—for it was no other—met my father, who had just had an audience of the prince, in a corridor of the castle and there stabbed him. There was no struggle; it was assassination, for my father's right hand was disabled by an old wound. And Pescara died innocent as surely as I hold you here; nothing could be further from his honest soul than intrigue and conspiracy. Was not this villainy? And yet perhaps Moncada thought that he was fulfilling a duty and acting as a good Christian in obeying the frown of a king. — Is it not horrible? Could such a thing have been done in your country, Charles?"

"In France? That depends. And yet — so coolly? No."

"Years after, when I had won my spurs, I met Moncada in the tent of my chief and father-in-law, Fabricius Colonna. He embraced me, called me his young hero, the rising star and hope of Spain, and he calmly examined my features. He said that I was like

my father whom he had known, and the blood froze in
my veins, for I was certain that it was Pescara's
assassin who had clasped me in his arms."

" And you allowed him to escape ?"

" That same evening I went out to take his life or
let him to take mine. He had disappeared. I could not
follow him up.   How could I find time for it — living
always in camp and in the midst of change ?   But the
spirit of my murdered father haunted me wherever I
went. — I learnt subsequently that the man I hated
had retired to a Carthusian monastery to expiate a
crime.   Then he reappeared on the other side of the
ocean, in the island of Cuba, where King Ferdinand
had granted him a rich estate, and he next went to
Mexico with the adventurous Cortes, I suspect as a
spy on that ambitious conqueror ; for Moncada lives
to carry out the ideas and schemes of his royal father.
He is in league with the fanatical Spanish party at
court which, happily, forms a counterpoise to the Bur-
gundians and Netherlanders.   On his return from
beyond seas he made a great merit of having preserved
New Spain for the crown by his secret influence, and
he is now respected and somewhat feared, even by the
emperor his nephew. — Now he is in Italy to crush or
ruin me.   This is Moncada."

" Do you know, Fernando," said Bourbon, who
had listened with interest, " I have long wished to do

you a service. Supposing I were to avenge your
father and release you from your foe at one blow?
Not by assassination; that is not my way, but in a
regular duel, for which I can easily find a pretext. I
do not risk my own life, for, with all respect to you,
you will admit that we French are better swordsmen
than you Spaniards. You are not implicated, and my
royal birth protects me. Will you have it so? I am
at your disposal." But Pescara answered with an
almost transfiguring light in his eyes: "No. It is too
late. I think differently now and leave the murderer
to the justice of the Eternal."

Bourbon looked amazed. Pescara took Ippolito
by the hand and said: "Now, we must not keep
madonna waiting any longer."

He stood aside for the duke. As they went down
stairs he asked the boy: "Are you already so devoted
to your mistress whom you never saw till to-day?"

"She was so kind to me at once," replied Ippolito,
"and she looked so like my sister whom I shall never
see again "— the ready tears trickled down his cheeks
— "for grandfather told me she had gone into a convent at Rome and taken the vows. And she used to
be so gay, poor Giulia; but lately she had been very
quiet, to be sure. How could she bear to bury herself
so young!" While he was speaking they reached the
garden.

"I beg you will introduce me to your illustrious wife," said Bourbon. "Not long since, in a book I opened, I found it said that nature had formed a perfect creature and then broken the mould that Vittoria Colonna might remain unique. You will allow me to see her?"

They made their way along the avenue of cypress and presently became witnesses, at some little distance, of an agitating scene: a female figure was dragging herself free from a man on his knees at her feet. At that moment Ippolito shrieked out: "There is that wicked magician: he will hurt madonna!" and he flew at his utmost speed to Donna Vittoria's assistance, while Morone sprang to his feet and vanished behind a laurel-hedge. The liberated lady came on flying feet to meet her smiling husband, with such a deep and girlish blush that Pescara thought he had never seen her look lovelier. Her dress was still fluttering though she was not even out of breath, as she said: "A suppliant laid wait for me and adjured me to lay his case before your excellency; he begs you not to let him wait too long for your decision as he is pining in suspense and expectancy."

"He chose his mediator wisely, Madonna," replied the marchese. "But everything in its turn. At this moment allow me to present to you his Highness the Duke of Bourbon." Vittoria, eager as she was, did not dissemble an expression of womanly interest.

The duke gave no sign of having been amused by the kneeling chancellor. He bowed respectfully, but with an air of refined pride, out of regard for Pescara, and also from that consciousness of ill-fame which never ceased to haunt him. He admired Vittoria's beauty without allowing his dark eyes to gaze long at her face or figure. He did not flatter her; he offered her no incense; he merely said: "I am happy in making the acquaintance of Madonna Vittoria, my friend's wife, and do her due homage." Then, walking on at her left hand, he fell into light and pleasant though trivial talk, and when she invited him to join them at supper he excused himself and took leave at the bottom of the villa steps with calm courtesy. Vittoria, modest as she was, had expected something more, if only from habit; for she was accustomed to the most extravagant adulation from all the celebrities of her time. But she smilingly disguised her disappointment, and went up the steps with her husband in the fast-falling dusk.

The meal was a short one, as Pescara preferred it so. Vittoria would allow no one to offer him the dishes but herself; he returned the compliment at dessert. Among the ices, fruit and sweetmeats, the confectioner had sewed up a crown made of almonds.

"Look," exclaimed Pescara, "here is something for my ambitious Vittoria!" He offered it to her, and her heart beat high.

When they rose they adjourned to the next room, where a chandelier shed a softened light, displaying the freshly-finished decorations. Children with gar-lands of flowers sported on the walls; the ceiling bore, in lozenges of gold, four heroic heads painted in grey monochrome — a singular quartette, lighted up by the hanging lamp: Aenaeas, King David, Hercules and Pescara. There was no furniture but an easy bench with a frame of chestnut wood, and on its back in carved letters were the words: " *Qui si conversa.*" "Here one must chat."

"How is it," asked Vittoria as she seated herself by Pescara's side, "that, in spite of his fine manners, the connétable impresses me unpleasantly — that, to speak plainly, he repels me?"

"Poor fellow!" said Pescara lightly. "Mars and the Muse, the rough and the refined, the hideous Leyva and the fair Vittoria, take equal offence at the son of the Capets, who has, nevertheless, done neither of them any harm, as I can testify. Some subtle influ-ence must steal in between him and those two persons, and I conclude that this distorting mist, this damaging cloud, is his treason — or whatever men choose to call his secession from his sovereign."

Vittoria turned a little paler.

"Treason. . . . . ."   Pescara dwelt on the syllables. "It is natural that a noble-souled woman should loathe the crime.   Whether I break faith with my friend or my trusting wife, or even with my fellow-conspirator — it is but a variety of the same base impulse. — The grand and gloomy poet, in whose pages you find refreshment for your soul, esteems betrayal as the blackest guilt, and in Giudecca his Cerberus, or Lucifer, gnashes a traitor in each of his three jaws. The first of them I know: it is he who kissed the Saviour.   But who are the others whom Lucifer has seized by the feet while their heads hang down ?   I cannot at this moment recollect.   Repeat the passage; you know the hundred cantos by heart."

Vittoria repeated :

> " Of th' other two,
> Whose heads are under, from the murky jaw
> Who hangs, is Brutus : lo !   Now he doth writhe
> And speaks not.   The other, Cassius, that appears
> So large of limb." *

---

* Carey's translation.

> Degli altri due, ch' hanno il capo di sotto,
> Quel, che pende dal nero ceffo, è Bruto :
> Vedi come si storce e non fa motto :
> E l'altro è Cassio, che par si membruto.
>
> —Inferno, CXXXIV.

The marchese went on composedly : " 'Brutus who doth writhe and speaks not,' is good; but — with all deference be it said — how could Dante describe Cassius, a man so lean that Julius declared he was frightened to behold him, as 'large of limb?' And tell me, Vittoria, what do you think of Cerberus' feast ?"

Vittoria responded bravely : " My lord, Caesar's assassins have no place in hell. In this I blame the poet."

" Impossible !" said Pescara mockingly. — " And yet you are right, my true Roman ! Fidelity is a virtue, but not the highest. The highest virtue is Justice."

And as Pescara juggled his wife away from the abyss, and the secret of his soul; and hindered her from getting the foothold which she longed for with all the vehemence of her nature to enable her to win the cause for which she had flown to Novara. Again and again did she seek a fresh road to the goal which Pescara took care that she should not reach. It now occurred to her that she might invoke the aid of the greatest living Italian patriot.

" It always surprises me, Pescara," she said, " that you, being the man you are, invariably prefer the more graceful to the powerful minds among our poets and painters : Ariosto and Raphael to Dante and his later

but equally great brother Buonarotti.   And yet you
yourself have a deep, reserved nature."

"It is for that very reason, Vittoria.   Art is a
thing for pleasure.   As to your Michael Angelo —
only beware of making me jealous of the broken-nosed
Cyclops whom you admire so much."

Vittoria smiled: "I have never seen his face, and
only know his work in the Sistina."

"The Prophets and Sibyls?   I saw them some
years ago and examined them carefully, but they have
vanished from my mind excepting a few details.   For
example, the man with his hair on end starting back
from a mirror. . . ."

"In which he sees the menaces of the present," she
eagerly interrupted.

"And a caryatid — crouching under a terrific bur-
den; a crouching, square, suffering figure.   The ugliest
woman, beyond question, as you are the loveliest. . . ."

"A crushed, oppressed, enslaved creature. . . ."

"I remember the Prophets too, now: Zachariah or
whichever it may be — bald, with his legs crossed;
Ezekiel scolding, in a turban; Daniel writing, writing,
writing.   Yes, and the Sibyls: the bent old woman
with a hawk's beak, her dim eyes poring into a tiny
book; and the one next her feeding her dying lamp
with oil; aye, and the most beautiful of all — the
young one with the Delphic tripod.   All wildly ener-

getic.   But what is the meaning of their frenzy?
What are they all preaching and prophesying?"

Vittoria broke out in flaming enthusiasm, as if she
herself sat in the council of the Prophets: "They are
bewailing enslaved Italy, and proclaiming the advent
of its deliverer and redeemer!"

"No," said Pescara with stern decision. "The
hour of redemption is past.   It is not mercy that they
foretell, but judgment."

Vittoria was chilled; but the look of judicial severity had already passed from her husband's features.

"Enough of the Chapel of the Prophets," he said
caressingly, "and of an art which shocks and terrifies.
— And you cannot have meant me when you spoke of
Italy's redeemer — though, to be sure, I have the
wound in my side," he added with one of those acrid
jests which he was apt to utter.

All Vittoria's tenderest feelings surged up at the
mention of that wound, which had filled her thoughts
day and night till Pescara had written to say that it
was healed.   She lovingly embraced him with her left
arm while with the other she stroked his waving
auburn hair low over his forehead, so that in the lamp-
light — and in her soothing presence — he looked
quite youthful.

It brought to her mind the memory of a day they
had spent together, not so very long ago.   It was at

one of her houses in the neighbourhood of Tarento. There, one evening when the scorching harvest-sun had set, in the glow of a darkening sky, they had each taken a sickle and, toiling with the still unwearied reapers, had each cut and bound a sheaf. She could see the great captain resting against his shock while she, improvising with facility, had taught the girls in the field a new song, such as are commonly sung in the south, which the young folks had not wearied of repeating till late at night. She reminded her husband of all this and it pleased him.

"Do you remember the song?" he asked.

"How should I?"

"Well, *mietitore* was made to rhyme with *suonatore*. There was not much in the song but a description of how the sheaves were carried in heaven with songs, as they are in the harvest-field. The simple ditty will still be sung by the people, I daresay, when I, and you after me, have long been silent. And I like it better, if I may say so, than a sonnet which came to me the other day in which you address me in a loftier style. Be calm, Vittoria! It is not yours. — I know it is not yours."

She flamed with indignation. "And who then has dared," she cried, "to assume my mask, and address you in my name? What audacious wretch? — But where is the forgery, that I may tear it to atoms?"

"Oh, that would be a pity! The verses would do you no discredit. — Here. . . ." And Pescara took a folded paper from his breast. She tore it open and went to stand under the lamp. She began reading with a panting bosom and hasty lips:

VITTORIA TO PESCARA.

"My name is Victory. I crown thy head
With laurels won in many glorious fights.
But woe betide if, straining Victory's rights,
I ever should my native land degrade!

Of Roman blood and ancient lordly race,
In my fair youth I proudly wedded thee;
Gave thee a home and civic dignity;
And in Italian eyes I lent thee grace.

And now I claim my guerdon for a life
Offered to thee, a flaming sacrifice.
My hero, what hast thou to give thy wife?

I know the spirits which within thee rise!
Use thy sharp sword as a releasing knife,
Free Italy, and let her be the prize!"

Never did a voice change more strangely under the impression of a poem; Vittoria had seized the sheet in anger, but she soon was mollified; then she read with feeling, and the last line came out with triumphant emphasis. She now frankly added:

"Yes, that is what I am and expresses what I hope, though I did not write it!"

Pescara looked up ironically. "The sonnet sounded wonderfully well from your lips," he said. "But it is a hollow performance and the offspring of an ignoble soul. Love asks for no reward, love gives itself unrequited, love makes no bargains. This is vulgar. No, Vittoria cannot have such thoughts. Those verses are the work of a hireling — and I know his name: his over-weening vanity has prompted him to raise the mask. Look here." And Pescara pointed out two tiny initials at the bottom right hand corner of the page: a P, and an A. "One of the 'divine' souls, as he calls himself! — I can see the Aretine with Giovanni de' Medici, his boon companion, the most profligate young fellow in all Italy; I can fancy them sitting together soaked with wine and sharpening each other's wit; and I can hear his blasphemous tongue: 'My word for it, Gian., it is no trifle to be wrapt up in the divine Vittoria,' — and a laugh of satyrs. — The Aretine laughs till he nearly rolls over, chair and all, — shakes and laughs open-mouthed. . . ."

"Perish the villain, the wretch!" exclaimed Vittoria with a sob; for Aretino and his doings were a matter of universal notoriety.

"Brava, my true Roman!" said Pescara applauding her. "But on one point he is right, sweetheart: your Christian name has fired your husband before now. It is a fine thing to be wedded to Victory!"

But she was not to be rallied any more. The very depths of her soul were revolted, the roots of her being were shaken; she was in tears, but glowing with fire and passion.

"But on another point he is wrong!" she cried vehemently. "For I do not know what spirits rise within you. I try in vain to read the secrets of your heart! You can play with your wife; you embrace me and put me aside. You are cruel; you have not even allowed me to deliver the message which I brought in all the joy of my heart."

"Because I have guessed it. — I blame his Holiness for having employed my noble wife as his servant, and for having beguiled you — who are truth itself — into carrying a message unworthy of you and of himself; a tissue of lies and sophistry which, within a day or two, I will compel him to withdraw and contradict. — His Holiness offers me Naples when I shall have conquered it, and absolves my conscience when I shall have stultified it. I have no faith in his power to bind and to loose in secular affairs, neither over me nor any other soul; nay," he added scornfully, "nor in spiritual matters either. All that is a thing of the past, since the teaching of Savonarola and the German monk."

"And Italy, my country, which you draw after you with magnetic power, is it to be wrecked on you?

Do you count it for nothing? Do you treat it with contempt?" cried Vittoria in despair.

The general answered mildly : " How could I treat a people with contempt who have given themselves into my hand? — But I will be frank with you : Italy appeals in vain and wastes its pains. I have long foreseen this temptation ; I saw it coming, gathering to a head like a rolling billow ; and I have not wavered, not for an instant, not in my lightest thought. For in truth I have no choice, I am not my own; I stand outside, apart."

Vittoria was alarmed.

" How? Are you not human? Are you a spirit and not flesh and blood? Do you not tread the earth you move on?"

" My guardian God," he calmly replied, " has stilled the storm that tossed about my helm."

" Your God!" cried Vittoria beseechingly as she threw her arms about him. " I will not leave you till you tell me who, then, is your God!"

Pescara gently released himself and replied with a look of suffering : " If you insist on it. — But come into the garden, I must have air."

They went out on the terrace; all the stars were bright above them, and a lonely twinkle of earthly hue was still to be seen in the old castle.

" There, the chancellor is watching, sleepless with dread and hope," she said compassionately.

"I think not," replied Pescara. "He is more likely to have read himself to sleep with some wrong-headed or worthless writer, and his low-burning lamp lights only the walls of his room."

He had guessed rightly. After some anxious hours, Morone had fallen asleep over Catullus.

Pescara took the path to the arbour with marble seats where he was wont to rest; they sat down under the leafy roof, clasping hands. Presently Vittoria whispered: "Now, speak to me!" But Fernando was silent. Steps were heard approaching, and another seat was taken by two persons conversing.

"Is that really the case with the general, Moncada? I can hardly believe it."

"Nor do I believe it yet, Leyva, but I am enquiring. As soon as I am certain I shall come forward and then we will act."

"What do you mean?"

"You shall collect your forces and we will seize him."

"He will defend himself."

"Then he will be beaten."

"And the emperor?"

"Do not be uneasy, his majesty has need of us; we are a match for him. — If you refuse to support me I must hire an assassin to kill him. Can I count upon you?"

"You may. . . . but it is a serious step. . . ." The other pulled him away: "I fancy," he said, "I heard some one breathing."

So it was. The damp night air had choked the listening general and caught his breath; he gasped a little. He now said: "We, too, will be going. The dew is falling and there is danger in the air." She clung to him.

Three blasts on the horn rang out from the castle.

"A courier," he said. "I shall have more papers to read this evening."

"Fernando," she said imploringly, "you are watched. The emperor suspects you. You are lost! Throw yourself into the arms of Italy. There lies your salvation, your only refuge!"

"I fear nothing," he replied. "The way is dark, but my refuge lies open to me."

They were now standing in the little entrance-hall of the villa, and Pescara awoke Ippolito who had fallen asleep on a bench.

"Go over to the castle," he said, "and bring me the despatch that has just arrived." Then he added, to Vittoria: "I fancy it will be from Madrid; a line from his majesty himself perhaps, for he sometimes writes to me without his ministers' cognizance. I am anxious still."

The castle town-clock was striking midnight with

weary, tremulous strokes, so slowly doled out that it
seemed a life time between them. The twelfth rang
out — past recall.

Ippolito tapped at the door and delivered a packet
which Pescara opened. It contained, among other
documents, an imperial rescript authorizing the march
on Milan, and empowering the field-marshal to deal
with the city, as his judgment and the circumstances
might dictate.

"Is that all?" asked Pescara. The boy humbly
bent the knee and handed him a note which he had
with difficulty persuaded the courier to entrust to him;
then he left the room. It was addressed:

" For the marchese's own hand."

" From the emperor," said Pescara opening it.
" Here, Vittoria, read it to me; he writes so closely."

She obeyed. There were but a few lines, as
follows:

" MY PESCARA :

" I, myself, have carried through this edict, grant-
ing you full powers, against my ministers. You have
many enemies. Beware of Moncada. I believe in
you, for I have prayed for you and saw an angel leading you by the hand. I have faith.

" YOUR KING."

Pescara smiled wearily.

"Charles' faith is too easy," he said. "It might bring him into trouble with another man than I. — But — how strange ! — He saw my Genius !"

"Tell me what, who is this Genius," Vittoria besought him. "I implore you, Pescara, — tell me."

"I believe that He is here," Pescara panted hoarsely. His breath came harder and sharper, he gasped and groaned. A fearful spasm oppressed his chest, and pressing his hand to his suffering heart he sank struggling for breath on an ottoman. Vittoria knelt down by him, supported and soothed him, suffering almost as much as he. She wanted to call Ippolito and send the boy for his grandfather the physician; but her husband forbade it by a sign. At last he fell asleep, utterly exhausted; indeed Vittoria had believed that he was dying. After drying her tears she, too, fell asleep, on her knees, her head in his lap. And then the lamp burned out.

CHAPTER V.

WHEN Vittoria woke her head was lying on a pillow and she was alone. The breath of dawn blew in through the open window. She started up to seek her husband, and found him walking up and down the terrace, refreshed by sleep and restored to life. She began to doubt that fearful struggle of the previous night; it seemed like a dream.

Pescara spoke at once. "Yesterday, sweet mistress, you asked me the name of my Genius and I could not bear to utter it to you. At length you almost wrung the secret from me, for it is difficult to keep anything from the wife one loves. And then He himself came and laid his finger on me. You know him now — His dread name may remain unspoken. — Nay, no tears! You shed them yesterday. Tell me now, where will you stay while I lead the emperor's army to take Milan."

"How could you conceal it so long from me, Fernando?"

"At first — but not for long — I concealed it from myself. . . . and yet, no: I knew my doom the evening of the fight at Pavia. My life set with that blood-stained winter sun. But knowing my end and the number of my days how could I bear to darken yours too soon? You have sometimes said to me that it is cruel to wake any one from happy sleep, and would never have it done. And I am not cruel."

"You are cruel," she replied, "or you could not have deceived me so bitterly; you would have sent for me and let me attend upon you."

"No one was to know it," he said.

"And your physician? He must have known of it, and I am wroth with him for having lied to me; I wrote to him and adjured him to tell me the truth."

"Poor Numa! He is grieved enough as it is, by his inability to cure me. He advised me to take a long rest in Ischia, but I told him it was in vain. — But why speak of all this? Where do you propose to remain, Vittoria?"

"Nay, Fernando, tell me all, do not conceal anything from me again."

"It is in vain, I said. The lung is pierced and that makes the heart suffer. Give me a respite only. Enable me to last through the summer, till autumn, till the first snow falls — so long as is necessary to complete my victory. But above all, said I, be secret. Let no one know the truth; it would treble the enemy's strength and ruin me and my army. Be silent, I say; I will have it so. — I insisted on it. — And I have acted life so well that Italy offers me the bridal ring!" He smiled. "And I shall sit on my horse once more. — But you, Vittoria, swear to me — nay, do not swear: you will do it for love of me — do not come hurrying after me, unless I send for you, through the dust of my march, across a country soaked in blood. And the whole warlike population would laugh at us, — not at you, who are so good and lovely,

but at the uxorious general. So you must remain
behind; but where? Here?"

Vittoria reflected, her face full of the deepest distress. Presently she said: "As I rode hither I came
past a small convent in the outskirts of the city. It is
called the Convent of the Sacred Wounds. I will stay
there till you need me, doing penance and praying for
your recovery."

"For my recovery?" he smiled. "Do so. And
you will not be too dull at the holy house. The convent, as I am told, has some beautiful voices and is
famous for its choir. — We will ride out there early;
now, while it is cool, and the dust on the high road
has not been kicked up in clouds."

He went across the park at a brisk pace to the old
castle, to order horses.

Vittoria followed more slowly, and seeing Numa,
who was on his way to enquire how the marchese had
passed the night, she went to meet him with a look of
sorrowful agitation; she meant to reproach him for
concealing the truth from her, and at the same time to
entreat him to prolong that beloved life by all the
mysteries and means of his science. But as he saw
her approaching the old man raised his trembling
hands in deprecation, conscious of his impotence, as
though to say: 'Spare me, I can do nothing!'

She understood the gesture and went on her way,

passing by Ippolito — who bowed humbly — without even seeing him to the boy's great distress.

In the castle-yard Pescara's heavy black charger was already standing in his splendid trappings, and by his side her own Arab, ready saddled. The general helped her to mount, and they rode out amid the rattle of drums in salute, across the drawbridge which fell before them and down to the endless rice-meadows of the plain of Lombardy. One of Pescara's squires followed them at a respectful distance, a Calabrian blackened by the southern sun; and with him, on a mule, rode Vittoria's Roman waiting-woman.

As they left the castle behind them its courtyard echoed with the unheeded cries of the forgotten chancellor. He awoke from bad dreams very early in the morning and had gone wandering about the garden, always finding himself stopped by walls and gates guarded by German or by Spanish men-at-arms. The Suabians were infinitely amused by his extraordinary gesticulations, while the Spaniards winked at each other, exchanging malicious glances: they did not doubt that the general had entrapped Morone in a snare, and promised themselves that next morning, when the army had gone forward, they would torture him to their hearts' desire and plunder him completely. At length he reached the circular arbour and sank exhausted on the very bench where, yesterday, he had found Pescara sleeping, and had stood watching him. At that moment he heard the salute of the man on guard at the drawbridge; he rushed to the castle yard and tried to get across. Held in check by the crossed halberts of the sentries, he could but wring his hands and watch Pescara and Vittoria as they disappeared in the misty distance.

It was a dull day after a bright one. There was not a breath of wind, not a sign of gathering clouds. Not a lark rose skywards, not a finch piped; the still dim light lay over the level fields. The convent soon came in sight and its peaceful walls slowly grew upon them. The husband and wife, to be sure, rode at scarcely more than a foot pace; the bereaved Vittoria in total silence; while, by a singular revulsion, the warrior's mind, now at rest, flew back on the light pinions of fervent love to his youthful days, and his fancy painted his grieving companion as an enchanting and lovely girl, a blossoming tender bride. Nor did he hesitate to remind her of the little events of those happy days; but he could not beguile her anxiety of a smile. He was now unburdened of his cruel secret, while she, suddenly and for the first time, was tasting its bitterness to the dregs.

They were now so close to the convent that they could hear the choir chanting in the chapel.

" What are they singing ?" he asked carelessly.

"A requiem, I think," she replied.

They dismounted at the gate, and to their surprise were met on the threshold by the abbess, followed by two serving sisters. She might have heard of their approach from some child perhaps, who had spied them from a hiding-place in the rice fields and run to announce them on bare, swift feet. The abbess had in fact learnt on the previous day that Donna Vittoria was at Novara, and had flattered herself that so pious and affable a lady would not leave "the Sacred Wounds" unvisited, for the convent possessed a greater distinction than even the highly-trained choir, in a mystical and ecstatic nun : Sister Beata, who bore the stigmata on her sickly and emaciated body. The energetic and sanguine superior had undertaken to make interest through Vittoria, whose influence over her husband was well known, for the remission of a heavy war-tax levied by Pescara — who was regarded by all the sacerdotal party of Italy as a godless and rapacious monster — on all monastic property, contrary to canon law and decent custom. But that the general, who usually avoided such sacred places, should himself accompany Madonna Vittoria, had never entered into the abbess' calculations.

A pleasant-looking woman with shrewd, dark eyes and pale, sweet features, she, welcomed the illustrious pair in a few well-chosen words. Then she stood in watchful silence, awaiting Pescara's reply and deeply impressed by his noble appearance.

"Reverend mother," the soldier said, "Donna Vittoria desires to enjoy a few days of pious peace in your convent during my absence on an expedition on which I start to-morrow, and which I expect to last about a week. She will stay with you till I bid her join me at Milan, when the fighting is over. Have you a suitable room to accommodate her?"

The abbess hastened to say that her own was at the marchesa's service.

"I require only a simple cell, like the humblest sister, with the usual fittings," said Vittoria; and the superior was surprised at her pallor, which, however she ascribed to natural anxiety for her husband in the field.

"When Donna Vittoria has settled herself," Pescara added, "let me know. I must speak with her again and beg to be allowed to see the convent and her cell. — As a special favour, for I wish your convent well. You will find me in the chapel." He bowed and left them.

Vittoria asked what the nuns had been singing. "A requiem," was the reply, "for the soul of Giulia Dati, the granddaughter of our aged physician; she died lately in Rome."

Then the abbess led the way, while two attendant

sisters went off to carry out her whispered instructions.

Pescara meanwhile was pacing up and down the chapel, his arms crossed over his breastplate; but he neither uncovered his head, nor went through any of the customary formalities of reverence. On his way back to Novara he was to meet his troops marching, according to orders, to assemble in that town, so he had put on his helmet and light armour, and trod the house of prayer and mortification with the air of a conquering hero.

"No," thought he to himself, but he did not speak. "This is the last time. I will part from her in life and vigour. I will spare her the sight of my sufferings. She shall see me again when I am at rest."

He believed himself to be alone, but he was being watched through the railing of the choir. The nuns, by the orders of the abbess had gone into the chapel again : she wished that Pescara should hear them singing. Even the mystic Beata had joined them, and her ecstatic eyes, with many a pair of brown and black ones, were fixed on the heroic figure with a devouring gaze. All these "brides of heaven" thought Vittoria a happy woman, envying her lot on earth; while she whom they esteemed so fortunate was sitting despairingly in a cell not far away, wringing her hands in anguish. Beata herself felt tempted to admire the proud lord of this world; but she conquered herself bravely, and fervently interceded with Heaven to bereave Vittoria of her idol for her soul's salvation. But this vehement instinct gave way to the more innocent movement of vanity. After a short whispered consultation the sisters triumphantly attacked their greatest achievement, a *Te Deum*, which was better suited to the conqueror of Pavia than any other chant or psalm. He would have listened, and he stood motionless in front of a large altar-piece representing the Redeemer dead upon the cross, of which the colours were still brilliantly new. But his eyes were riveted not on the divine Head, but on the soldier who had thrust his lance into the sacred side. He was obviously a Swiss: the painter must have studied the dress and attitude of such a man with singular exactitude, or have painted it from the life. The soldier stood with his legs apart, the right in black and the left in yellow, and was giving a shrewd thrust from below with his gloved hand. Helmet, gorget, cuirass, arm and thigh-pieces, scarlet hose, broad-toed shoes, all was complete; but it was not the dress with which he was so familiar that attracted the great captain, but the head that was set on the bull-neck: small blue eyes as clear as crystal, snub-nose, a grinning mouth, a fair crisply curling moustache, a dark complexion with fresh red cheeks, ear-rings shaped like a milk ladle and a curiously mingled expression of candour and cunning.

The black and yellow trunks marked him as a native of Uri, and Pescara, with the habit of identification of a leader of men, at once remembered that he had seen this very man before — a small, but broadshouldered and lithe figure — but when and where? Suddenly a sharp pain, like a stab, shot through his side, and he knew at once who the man was: It was the Swiss who had run him through with a lance at Pavia! Not a doubt of it. As he received the thrust from the enemy who had stooped low to the ground, his eyes had for an instant met those keen eyes, and he had seen that grin of satisfaction. After this identification the unexpected incident made no further impression on Pescara: he turned to the abbess, who had come to fetch him, and asked who had painted the picture.

"Two Mantuans," she replied, looking down a little, "gifted young fellows, but of very doubtful morals. The nuns had been glad indeed to see the last of them."

When Pescara opened the door of the cell Vittoria was on her knees. Unwilling to disturb her, he waited a few minutes in silence looking through a window in the arched alcove, where he found a seat on the sill, out on the turfed mounds and graveyard crosses; at length, however, he said: "What are you doing, Vittoria?"

" Penance," she replied.

" For what ?"

She rose and said, with hands still clasped : " For myself, and for you, and Italy. — For Italy's criminal pride and monstrous sins, by which she must perish since you are the only man who could have saved her. For myself, because I came to lead you into temptation. For you, because you would fain quit this earth. I have prayed for your immortal part — but Heaven has not yet heard my prayers." And she shook her head mournfully.

He drew her down on to the window-seat, and took her hand as a brother might his sister's. A longing came over him to pour out his heart to her, whether it was that the secret that had lain between him and his wife was removed, or an unconscious impulse to prolong this last interview.

"Oh, those of little faith !" he began lightly. "Leave me to my dark deliverer. As a boy I believed, like my mother who was a saint, in all the Church prescribes; now I see around me the great river of Eternity. The angel of death came very near me even in my first battle, where he chose my comrade in arms — your brother, Vittoria — to fall without a sound, a ball through his heart. I have slain many a hecatomb in His honour, and he has greeted and laid a finger on me again and again, almost on every battlefield, — for it would seem that I am more vulnerable than other men. But time has taught me to love the Reaper. In those weeks after Pavia, when I first knew that he had marked me, I rebelled and raged and resisted like a refractory boy. But by degrees I began to think — and now I am sure — that He knew the right hour. The knot of my life is inextricable: He will cut it."

Vittoria, pale and rigid, hung on his lips, staring blankly as if she saw a splendid palace in flames and every capital lighted up by the blaze.

" I tell you, wife," he went on, "my path leads downwards. I go down before Victory and Fame. Even if I had not my wound, still I could not live. In Spain envy, foul calumny, uncertain court favour — soon to be undermined, disgrace and a fall; and here, Italy has only hatred and prison for him who has disdained her. If I had betrayed my emperor I should have died — of myself, of my broken faith; for I have two souls in me, one Spanish and one Italian, and one would have killed the other. Nor, indeed, do I believe that I could have created a living Italy. It bears aloft the radiant lamp of Genius, it is true; but in the exuberant joy of its vain existence it has rebelled against eternal laws. It must do penance: you are right, Vittoria: it must learn in fetters to be free. — Still, this Spanish empire, whose gloom is spreading with lurid smoke on both sides of the sea, fills me with horror: Slaves and executioners. I can detect the hideous taint in myself. And, most horrible of all: I know not what monkish madness! Your Italy, with all its sins, is human."

Vittoria's eyes brightened when she saw that Pescara loved Italy.

"You would have given her freedom, and with freedom, virtue!" she exclaimed; but her husband went on as if he had not heard her.

"As it is, I am snatched from the melée. I am delivered; and I believe that my deliverer means well by me, and will lead me away with all gentleness. Whither? — To rest. — Now let us part, Vittoria." He was about to kiss the tears from her eyes, but his lips met the tenderest lips.

"Yet one thing I must say," he went on. "Let the world judge me as it will. I am beyond the gulf. — Farewell. Do not see me off. Come to me at Milan, but not till I send for you." Vittoria promised —but not to keep her word.

When Pescara took leave of the abbess she had no need to formulate her petition. The general granted the remission of the war tax as a matter of course in return for the asylum offered to his wife. There was such joy in the convent at this happy issue from a pecuniary difficulty and short commons, that the sisters covered their guests' table with their choicest confectionery. But Vittoria's place was empty.

Pescara rode slowly back to the city towers, followed by the blessings of the sisterhood. His fiery black charger wondered at this easy pace; shrill, martial music rang across the plain, as troops, marching in every direction, announced the opening campaign. He snorted as though he already sniffed the scent of powder, and ambled proudly, as though conscious of bearing victory.

"It is hard to part," thought the captain. "I would not have to do it again." — Once more had life forced itself upon him and his arms had held the best it had to give: beauty and high-heartedness. Youth had fired up within him, and for a few minutes after his edifying words to Vittoria his spirit rebelled against annihilation. The noble blood which flows in mortal veins, the sense of energy revolted against eternal peace. His bright grey eyes flashed with rage against his murderer, whose picture he had seen, and he struck his breast with his mailed right hand as though to crush the wasp that had stung him; his horse whinnied and broke into a short canter, either spurred by an unconscious touch of his master's heel, or because they were in such perfect sympathy that the steed was aware of his rider's vexed humour.

Riding along in this mood, Pescara watched the varying fortunes of a fierce fray in a rice field which was being trampled into mud. A man was defending himself single-handed against overpowering numbers. A shabby little fellow, in tattered black and yellow was madly fighting a dozen Spaniards with the stump of a broken spear. He had felled two, but was now no match for the rest, and a sword was already at his throat when the soldier kneeling over him was dragged back by another, who pointed to Pescara, now rapidly approaching. At a sign from their chief the party followed him, with their prisoner, under the shade of a huge oak by the side of the road, the only tree far and wide on the sweltering plain. Pescara dismounted and leaned against the mossy trunk. He was panting from the swift ride and this pause was opportune, giving him time to compose himself and rest under the pretext of an enquiry.

The officer of the Spanish patrol reported that he had seen a Swiss running off through the corn, probably a fugitive from Pavia who had been lurking somewhere about till now, and had captured him in case he should be a Milanese spy. Having ended his statement the peaked-bearded Spaniard fixed his eye on a sturdy bough which grew horizontally from the oak-tree.

Pescara bid the Spaniards withdraw and stand on

guard at some little distance, and then eyed the Swiss from top to toe. Rusty as his armour was, and his trunk-hose in rags, the general at once recognized the costume represented in the convent-picture, nay, and those keen little eyes; while the face of the culprit before him even expanded to the same broad grin, whether out of sheer fright, or because he recognized the great captain.

"Pick that up and give it to me," said Pescara pointing to the broken spear-shaft which one of the soldiers had flung at the prisoner's feet as evidence of the wounds inflicted on his comrades. It was the armed half of the lance, and the head was bloody. The man obeyed and Pescara felt the point with his finger; then he flung the stump away.

"What is your name?" he asked.

"Blasi Zgraggen, of Uri," was the answer.

Pescara made no attempt to repeat this unpronounceable surname, which seemed to have come direct from the ragged peak of an Alpine mountain; he only italianized the fellow's Christian name: "Biagio," said he, "you have wounded two of my men; I think I will have you strung up here."

Blasi Zgraggen replied: "If you have me hanged it will not be for this last deed, but because. . . ."

"Silence!" ordered the general. He could be revenged by letting the laws of war take their course,

but such revenge could not be allowed either to himself or to his victim. " How did you happen to be
left behind?" he asked. Zgraggen, who spoke the
Lombard dialect with ease, began boldly: " I was
wounded and ridden down at the battle of Pavia, and
there I lay, my broken lance by my side. At night I
dragged myself to the hills, hungry, and begging my
way. My lord, do you see a long red roof out there,
to the right of the poplars? There lives Narracivallia
with her husband. He gave me some field-work; till
the war is over I cannot get across the frontier. Presently Narracivallia began to make eyes at me. Then,
in a dream I saw my father and my two grandfathers,
who all live at home, though the old folks are very
feeble now. First came father, and shook his finger at
me and said: ' Take care what you are about, Blasi!'
Then came his father and folded his hands and said:
' Think of your soul, Blasi.' Last of all came mother's
father and he pointed to the door and said: ' Run,
Blasi!' and I shot out of bed and looked for my
clothes. Narracivallia had talked me out of my silk
gloves and my chain-stitched cravat to make a fine
show in church. — I had still only half my wits about
me, and lost even those when I went into the convent
chapel at dawn for Angelus, and — think of my terror
— saw myself, as large as life, thrusting my spear into
God's body."

" Ah !" said Pescara with a smile.

" A rascally shame !" said Zgraggen angrily. "You must know, my lord, that a couple of painters had been wandering round here a little while since, and had come to the farm one day for a glass of milk. One of them fixed his eye on me: 'The very man we want,' said he, looking at my black and yellow clothes. 'Fetch your spear and armour, man.' I did as he asked me. Then the painter tells me to straddle my legs, straddles his too, and has me just as I am on a piece of canvas. Then the rascals promise me that my likeness shall come to great honour, and they put me in the convent piercing the Redeemer !"

Pescara felt an impulse of benevolence to the blunt-spoken fellow : "Take this," he exclaimed in a sudden caprice, and held out his full purse to the man of Uri. Blasi took it in his right hand and counted out the gold pieces into his left, gravely meditating. Then he pocketed the ducats and offered the purse back again.

" Keep it : the slides are gold." The Swiss stowed the purse on the top of the ducats.

" Where am I to be posted, my lord ?" he asked. He could only suppose that Pescara meant to employ him and that this was earnest money.

Pescara replied : " I have not hired you ; and it seems to me that after three such solemn warnings you had best go back to your own home and earn an honest living."

"Then what makes you give me so much money when I have done nothing to serve you?" said Zgraggen. "On the contrary, much to hurt you?" he added in his own mind. Such a return from Pescara transcended all his powers of imagination and aggrieved his honesty.

"Magnanimity!" said Pescara laughing.

Blasi had never heard the word. It occurred to him, however, that it must mean grand doings and as in camp he had often seen spendthrifts flinging away their money by handfuls, this soothed him. "To be sure," said he.

Pescara signed for his horse to be brought up. "And to insure your safe journey," said the warrior, with one foot in the stirrup:. "Take this, too." He tossed him a permit, and Zgraggen was within an ace of thanking him — contrary to the custom of his countrymen. At least he would wish his lordship a long life: but as he looked up at Pescara he saw sickness too plainly stamped on that face, with his keen Swiss eyes, which could not be deceived by the spiritual vitality which cheated others. He involuntarily spoke the wish: "God grant you a joyful resurrection, my lord!" And then, shocked at his own speech and its evil augury, he ran off across the fields

with his spear-stump, which he had carefully picked
up and now used as a staff. The Spaniards had
looked on in amazement; the old officer shaking his
head with superstitious doubtfulness over his chief's
generosity — he was usually such a thrifty man.

The men who had captured the Swiss formed part
of the army-corps which was now approaching in a
cloud of dust to the rhythm of beating drums. Pescara rode forward to meet his brave men, and was
hailed with shouts of joy; then he took his place
behind the drummers and in front of the first company,
whose captain respectfully made way.

For some time he rode alone at the head of his
troops. Then a horseman in a white cloak came out
from Novara and joined him. They rode side by side
into the castle gate. Pescara's companion followed
him in silence and entered his room close behind him.

Pescara turned round.

" What do you want, Moncada ?" he asked.

" An interview in strict privacy; and you will not
refuse me a second time."

" I am at your service."

" Your highness," Moncada began, " I have, with
your permission, spoken to the chancellor. He was
pale and terrified, and assured me with a thousand
oaths, that he had come here to obtain some delay and
easier terms — that nothing else had brought him to

Novara. Then he talked in the wildest way—like a bad conscience. That man is a fathomless pit of lies; the eye loses itself in its depths. I am confident that he is here on the League's business."

"Just so," said Pescara.

"And that he has offered you the position of its chief?"

"Just so."

At this moment there was a noise in the ante-room. The chancellor thrust Ippolito out of his way and rushed into the room with crazy haste, a frantic look, and staring eyes. Close at his heels came Bourbon and del Guasto, both already with their armour on, vainly endeavouring to keep him back. He threw himself in despair at Pescara's feet; Moncada slowly shrank into the background.

"My Pescara!" cried the terrified man, "patience has its limits! I can bear this torture no longer. Every minute lasts an eternity. I am dying of it. Be merciful and give me your answer."

Pescara replied very calmly: "Forgive me, Chancellor, for having kept you waiting; my time was not my own. But I was just about to send for you. Your speech yesterday gave me much to think about—for the fate of a nation is no trifle—but pray be seated I cannot talk when you are gesticulating so vehemently." Morone convulsively clutched the back of a chair.

"I have weighed the matter; — but first of all Chancellor, let us put everything personal out of the question. You and I quite apart: Does Italy at this moment deserve to be free, and is she capable — such as she now is — of accepting and maintaining her freedom? I say no." He spoke deliberately, as if weigh-ing each word in the scales of justice.

"Freedom has twice flourished in Italy, at two different periods. First at the beginning of the Roman republic, when the welfare of the state was all in all. Then in those glorious commonwealths, Milan, Pisa and others. But at present she is on the threshold of slavery, for she is lost to all honour, and bereft of every virtue. In such straits no one can help and save — neither monk nor God. — How is her lost freedom to be regained? Only through a shock and ferment of moral forces proceeding from the deep heart of the people. Somewhat as they are just now in Germany, conquering the faith, by the fires of hatred and of love. — But hers? Where in all Italy shall we find — I will not say faith and conscience, for these with you are quite out of date — but simply right-mindedness and conviction? Not even honour and shame are to be found among you — nothing but shameless self-seeking. Of what are you Italians capable? Seduc-tions, treason, assassination! On what do you rely? On favouring circumstances, the dice of chance, the

fluctuations of politics.   No nation can be founded or
reconstructed on such bases.   Verily, Chancellor, I tell
you plainly," — and Pescara raised his voice as if to
pronounce judgment — " Your Italy is as perverse and
fantastical as you yourself and your conspiracy."

" The truth !"   It was Moncada who spoke.

" Even the hero you have selected, Morone, is on
the eve of death."

But these last words of Pescara's were lost in a
louder outcry.   Morone had hastily looked round and
discovered Moncada ; seeing his scheme thus revealed
to the Spaniard he fell into a fury, his features were
quite distorted and he raged like one possessed.

" False and cruel, false and cruel !   Oh, I was as
one struck blind !"   Then, raving with wild thirst for
revenge, he shrieked to Moncada :

" Listen, Cavaliere — it was he," and he pointed to
the general, " he is the guilty man !   The whole conspiracy was on his account !   I am but his tool and
now the monster sacrifices me !"

The duke at this moment stepped forward ; he had
been standing with del Guasto behind Pescara, enjoy-
ing this vehement scene : " *Saute, Paillasse mon ami,
saute pour tout le monde*," he said mockingly to
Morone   " If only we had not happened to be listening, both of us, behind that red curtain with gold
tassels ! — I must tell you about that some day ; it will

make you die of laughing. Did you not hear me whistle at you?" Then, with sudden gravity, he fixed his eyes on Moncada, laid his hand on his heart, and said: "By my royal blood, the marchese did not swerve by a hair's-breadth from his honour and fidelity, at the meeting yesterday."

Morone was annihilated. Del Guasto laid a hand on his shoulder and drew him away with him. "Consider, my lord chancellor," he said, "our eaves-dropping has saved you from the rack."

The duke, too, left the room in obedience to a look of entreaty from Pescara.

"Your highness," Moncada said, "I am convinced. You were but mocking this man, with more condescension perhaps than beseems Spanish pride. Pescara cannot conspire with such a thing as he. Still, Sir, the liar spoke the truth in his impotent rage when he accused you of being the leader of the Italian conspiracy — or not the leader, but the encourager. By not repressing it you have fostered and matured it. It would have been easy for you to speak a decisive word and to put a stop to it by a single indignant and conspicuous gesture. This you have not done. You stood still, a dark and distinct figure."

"Cavaliere," Pescara put in, "I owe no account to you of my actions, only to my sovereign the emperor."

"Your King," retorted Moncada. "Due respect

requires you to call him so, for the King of Spain is greater than the emperor. And Ferdinand's grandson will be King of Spain. Charles develops slowly, and is still subject to various and varying influences, but his Spanish blood will assert itself and absorb the German in him to the last drop. He hates heresy, and his piety will keep him a Spaniard." He spoke with a quiet smile and ecstatic light in his eyes. — " Avalos," he went on, " your forefathers fought for the faith against the Moors till your ancestor sailed for Naples with Alfonso. Be faithful to your origin. In your veins flows the noblest blood of Spain, and how can you, who love what is great, hesitate between the universal dominion of Spain and the contemptible little Italian powers? The earth is ours, as it once was Rome's. Note the wonderful ways of God: Arragon and Castile joined in marriage, Burgundy and Flanders on our side, the imperial dignity won, a new world discovered and conquered, and, to hold and rule all this, a people inured to war, whose sacred sword has twice been steeped in heathen blood! All that this wretched man can give, Spain offers you a thousand-fold: treasures, lands, fame — and Heaven! — For we fight for Heaven, and for the Catholic faith, that there is but one Church on earth — or else God would in vain have become man. Foreseeing how in these latter days Hell would defile the Apostolic chair and disgorge its last heresy — this German monk — He created the Spaniard to purify the throne of St. Peter and exterminate the heretic. To this end He has given the world into our hands, for everything earthly has a heavenly purpose. — I have long thought of these things in my Sicilian monastery, and dreamed that I myself was to be the chosen instrument of this spiritual warfare; but then his face was revealed to me — the face of that Other, the Elect. I was unworthy of such an honour by reason of my sins, and I came forth into the world again."

Pescara was silent; he gazed at the crazy visionary.

"But I work too, while it is yet day. Not a year since, I stood behind Hernando Cortes when the devil showed him from a mountain-top the golden towers of Mexico, just as he now shows you, Pescara, the glories of Italy. This hand held back the waverer; and I now put it forth against you, Pescara, to keep you a true son of Spain, for Spain is the Universe and under the protection of Ferdinand the Catholic who sits in glory."

Pescara broke silence: "Do not name that man," he cried. "He killed my father."

Moncada sighed deeply.

"Do you repent?"

Moncada struck his breast with contrition and muttered to himself: "My sin, my sin! — Unconfessed and unabsolved."

Pescara perceived that this penitent did not regret the murder, but only that he should have committed it on one who was unprepared: "Depart from me!" he cried.

Moncada withdrew to the threshold like a man aroused from a dream. Then he collected himself and said: "Forgive me, Excellency! I was absent in the spirit. One word more in all sobriety: I do not know your aim and end. Whatever it may be, you will take Milan; that first step commits you neither to fidelity nor infidelity. I await the second, to see whether you depose the duke and punish arrogance. If you do not, it is treason to Spain and your king!" — And he vanished.

Pescara withdrew and took some food. Then he received the duke and del Guasto and gave them his last orders. He spent the remainder of his time to spare in looking through his private papers; a world of wickedness gathers and closes round a man in power. He destroyed most of them; his death should injure no man. He had had a charcoal brasier brought in and burnt the letters in its blue flame. By the time he had finished this business his tapers were half consumed; it was near midnight. Pescara folded his arms over his breast, and sat lost in such deep thought that he did not hear the step of a man who stole into the room.

A voice said: " What is your end, Avalos ?"

He saw Moncada.

Pescara put his hand into the brasier, now dead and cold, closed it and held it out to Moncada.

" My end ?" he said, and opened his hand: Dust and ashes.

———

Loud alarms on the drum now rang through the castle; every one was astir. The general bid his servants fit his armour on. When he went out into the paved hall, in the flickering torchlight, reflected from glittering spears and breast-plates, he saw in the courtyard, his black charger, splendidly harnessed and striking sparks from the stones with his impatient hoofs; and by his side a litter between two easy-paced palfreys. He had órdered both to be brought out, leaving the choice till the last moment. He sighed as he got into the litter to conceal the sufferings which he felt coming on, and was borne away through the gate, while his neglected war-horse plunged with rage and threw the groom who tried to mount him. He had to be led after his master.

Then the hapless chancellor was brought forth. Spanish soldiers crowded round him, robbed him of his chain, his rings, and his purse, and mounted him, not

on his own handsome mule from the royal stables of
Milan, but on a miserable ass, and riding backwards,
cruelly placing the poor brute's tail in his fettered hands.
Then they, too, marched out through the gate with
diabolical laughter, in which the chancellor joined out
of sheer despair.

CHAPTER VI.

MEANWHILE, in the castle of Milan, which from
a stronghold of joy had become the abode of terror, Sforza was spending miserable days and still more
wretched nights, helplessly and vainly clamouring for
his chancellor. He had had a visit from del Guasto,
who had come to announce to him that his chief had
some little time back received the chancellor of Milan.
But he, instead of the confession Pescara had expected,
had imparted to him, in his grace's name, schemes
which were as wild as they were wicked. These had
determined the general to march on Milan without
delay — as indeed he had already threatened — and to
treat his grace as guilty of high treason. Del Guasto
had enjoyed the duke's alarm, and had vanished again
from the city. The imperial army was advancing by
rapid marches, and even when it was within sight of

Milan the timorous duke was still hesitating between
surrender and resistance when he was snatched back
into the path of honour by a handful of brave nobles
of Lombardy, and also by a sudden impulse of warlike
feeling — of which his grandfather's blood could not be
wholly incapable. He donned a suit of artistically
wrought armour and crowned his feeble head with a
helmet of the finest chiselled work.

It is a fact that he was standing on the great bas-
tion at the moment when Pescara led his troops on to
storm the town. In a trembling voice the duke
ordered his picked musketeers to fire. When the
smoke blew away the field was strewn with Spaniards.
Pescara moved among the wounded and the dead with
a few more at his side, and still at some distance ahead
of the crowd of his followers hurrying after him under
del Guasto's lead. He wore no armour. He had lost
his helmet, and his dark-hued mantle fluttered in
tatters. Dressed in bright red, he walked on calmly
and steadily, flourishing a gleaming two-handed sword,
It was as though Death in person were marching in
wrath against the fortress; and as, at this juncture, the
bad news was spread that Bourbon had taken the
southern gate, and Leyva was storming the north wall,
pale fear fell upon the garrison. The reloaded cannon
remained unfired, the officers who threw themselves in
front of their terror-stricken men were trodden down,

and the duke himself was swept on before the frantic
fugitives.

On his return to the palace, as he wandered aim-
lessly into the throne room the canopy of the throne
fell to the ground before his eyes, with its hangings of
gold brocade patterned with lions and eagles. In the
general confusion the ducal upholsterer had made his
way to the throne room and loosened the splendid tissue to carry it off; but hearing the approaching tumult,
he had made his escape. The duke, startled by so evil
an omen, threw himself in despair on a chair, cover-
ing his face with both hands, expecting his fate and the
conqueror.

He had not long to wait. There was a brief, iron
clatter of arms — the Swiss body-guard, who had remained faithful, were being slaughtered or disarmed —
and Pescara came in, bare-headed and without his
sword, followed by Charless of Bourbon, in full armour
with his helmet on, and a weapon in his blood-stained
hand. He had been the first to mount the scaling-
ladder, and had been thrown with it into the moat, but
without being seriously wounded. The marchese
bowed to his conquered foe who struggled on to his feet.

"Your highness need not be uneasy," said Pescara.
"I come not as an enemy, but to claim your allegiance to your suzerain, the emperor."

Sforza looked up at him. Seeing neither scorn nor

vengeance in the thoughtful features, but rather sympathetic insight and clemency, the helpless boy burst
into tears and stammered out:

"I have always been true to his majesty at heart;
he has no more devoted servant or truer vassal; but I
was led astray, miserable creature that I am, led into
evil — my diabolical chancellor. . . . I did not even
command this armed resistance. — I was pushed,
urged — by Valabrega and a few other nobles. . . .
By all the apostles and martyrs I am no Italian
patriot, only the most cruelly coerced of princes, in the
most impossible position !"

This total abjection in the descendant of two such
heroes as his grandfather and greatgrandfather seemed
to pain Pescara. However, he let his confession have
its course; but avoided, out of respect, giving the
youth his hand which he tried to take when his speech
was ended. He was afraid that in his utter abasement
the duke might kiss it.

During this scene of self-humiliation, which at the
bottom of his heart he was keenly relishing, Charles of
Bourbon standing behind Pescara, had signed to a
page to fetch him a cup of wine and drank it off in
long gulps.

"Your highness," said Pescara, "my powers are
absolute. If you are thoroughly convinced that you
have drifted into a mistaken and dangerous game, if

you can make up your mind with a firm will to seek
safety henceforth where it is to be found — under the
emperor, and never to swerve, I take the responsibility
of promising you pardon, and will clasp hands upon it.
Your highness may believe me: you will in any case
fare better with the emperor than with the League."

But he at once detected that such unexpected
leniency had made Sforza suddenly distrustful, that the
lad, whom fate had taught to be suspicious, fancied he
scented guile, and that his hand trembled and was
half withheld.

"Your highness may trust me," he said with emphasis. "The emperor and I keep our word."

Sforza put out his hand, and the conqueror added
kindly: "I know how painful your highness' position
must be, and — if I may speak plainly — how your
spirit has been wounded and crushed by an unhappy
boyhood. Your first need is stability. By walking
and taking patience in the path laid down by his
majesty you will escape the shocks of the storms of
the times. I myself," he added less sententiously, and
in a tone almost of affection, "have always been
devoted to your highness out of gratitude to my
models, your two noble ancestors — though both of
them," and he laughed, "robbed me of many a night's
sleep in my young days. There is a charm and an
incentive in manliness and magnanimity."

Francesco Sforza was comforted by this friendly demeanour, but he asked in some alarm: " And I shall still be duke? Give me your word, Pescara."

" My solemn word. If I have the smallest influence with the emperor, and if you can confirm your soul."

" And — no harm shall befall my chancellor?"

" I believe none, your highness."

" He may still be my minister?"

Pescara could not forbear smiling at the inseparability of this couple. " But your highness forgets that you but now spoke of Girolamo Morone as the worst of councillors. I should advise you to request his majesty to appoint another and wiser head to this difficult office. There are plenty in Italy; it need not be a Spaniard."

" No, no, your grace! Your chancellor will not get out of this scrape! That Helen is my share of the spoil," said Bourbon speaking for the first time.

Sforza gazed at him in terror. " He, here?" he groaned. " He wants my Milan! He has long dreamed of that. Help me, mighty Pescara!"

At this Bourbon angrily dashed the crystal cup on to the marble floor, as if he were dashing himself to pieces; it flew into a thousand fragments with a sharp crash; " Your highness," he said, " there lies my dukedom of Lombardy."

As the glass sherds scattered Moncada came in with Leyva, who was covered with dust and blood from head to foot.

"My lord," said Moncada, "I congratulate you on this victory, fought with no less valour than the many former battles you have won. I have been, as beseems me, in the anteroom; then I heard drinking and laughter in here; and when Leyva came in, after taking the north gate and earning his drink too, I ventured to come in — and at the right moment I think. For it seems to me that judgment is being pronounced, and my lord of Bourbon is expressing symbolically to this traitor-duke the ruin he has deserved. But do not be so violent, my lord! I imagine that the general will call a court-martial, on which I may claim a seat and vote as a devoted servant of the royal house. A provisional court, of course, pending a decision from Madrid."

Pescara was quite calm.

"I do so," he replied. "I appoint my two colleagues, his highness of Bourbon and Leyva, the assessors. I will preside. You, Cavaliere, I must exclude, since you hold no appointment. Here are my credentials," and he drew the imperial rescript out of his red doublet.

Moncada seized the document and read: "As his judgment and the circumstances may dictate — hm.

Your excellency will allow me. — This imperial authorization seems to say that full powers to enforce any measures, whether in matters civic or military, as you may think proper so long as they do not in any way prejudice the rights and interests of his Catholic majesty. — I therefore will remain as a silent but watchful witness."

" So be it," said Pescara patiently.

Leyva now came forward and desired that Girolamo Morone should be sent for. " He is in the palace," he added. " I saw him brought in amid the hooting and dirt-throwing of the populace of Milan who lay all their griefs at his door."

Pescara gave the order.

There was an uncomfortable pause. The embarrassed servants placed seats, and brought in the ducal chair with its crown and coat of arms for their impeached lord; when Morone came in, bearing many marks of ill-treatment, he saw the three generals seated in judgment, Pescara in the middle; and opposite to them his duke.

" Courage, Francesco," he whispered as he took his accustomed place by his side. " Lay everything on me."

Pescara spoke.

" His highness of Milan declares that he holds fast to his fidelity to his liege lord, that he only fell away from it for a time, and appeared to be acting criminally under the suggestions of that man."

The duke nodded:

" It is so. I confess that I am guilty," said the chancellor without flinching.

" His highness moreover asserts that he did not command that Milan should resist the imperial arms; on the contrary, he declares that this was the unlicensed act of a few rebellious Lombards; and I think it is credible. — What is your opinion, Leyva?"

Leyva wrinkled his hideous face and growled out: " Francesco Sforza is guilty of felony and proved so by the bare facts. He should be kept in close guard. The emperor, in my opinion, will depose him, and have him carried to Spain."

" And what is your verdict?" Pescara turned to Bourbon.

The constable was playing with his torn glove and he said in a melodious voice: " His highness was misled by that amazing trickster who bewitched me too, once, and many more, till he found his master in our general. But the duke seems to me to have come to his senses, and I am of opinion that it is neither desirable nor needful to inflict the indignity of imprisonment on him, since the city is in our hands. His highness of Milan may remain free."

" Two votes to one, since that is my opinion,"

Pescara decided.   Moncada crossed his arms and said
nothing; Leyva, whose deep scar looked as though
suffused with blood, twisted his moustache; Bourbon
rose, offered Sforza his arm and led him out of the
room.

Outside he met del Guasto, who murmured to him
that it was strange, but Leyva's troops were marching
on the palace.   Bourbon knit his brows.   " Watch
and report!" he commanded.

Del Guasto was flying off again but shouted over
his shoulder: " And I hear that Donna Vittoria is at
the gate, and asking for the general."

When Bourbon went back into the throne room
Leyva was insisting on imprisonment and the rack,
and after full confession, the block and axe for Morone, who stood as pale as death.

"The rack!" he moaned.   " If you wring me like a
wet cloth you can get nothing out of me but blood
and sweat.   I have confessed fully to the general —
you are not cruel, Pescara."

" Pooh, Pescara!" cried Bourbon resuming his seat.
" Do you think the Lord will find any pleasure in the
grimaces of that foolish face?   I will not allow it.   I
will not have my Morone racked and wrung.   Do not
be afraid, Girolamo; not a hair of your head shall be
hurt : you shall be my secretary.   My merciful sentence is that Girolamo shall remain in his own house,

under watch and ward, till I have asked the emperor to hand him over to me."

"That seems to me quite adequate," said the general. "Morone has confessed before three trustworthy witnesses of whom I am one. No unnecessary torture, but safe keeping. Two votes to one. Take him, your highness. I suspect that Girolamo Morone will once more turn his coat and serve the emperor."

Morone, wild with joy at this respite from death and the torture chamber, exclaimed:

"Pescara! Italy cannot exist without you! That is at an end! Do with me what you will, I am the creature of your generosity and kindness. And if anything more is to be said, let me tell you, my lords, — and this accounts for everything — that the League sprang from the brain of his Holiness, like Athene from Jupiter's. . . ." Suddenly he was silent, but only for an instant, as he caught sight of a dignified looking man in travelling dress who had just come in. Then he promptly added: "No one knows it better than this man." It was Guicciardini, whose eyes glanced inquiringly round the circle but rested at last on Pescara's face.

"I am intruding, my lord?" he said. "But I will be brief. I come as express courier from his Holiness, who on this occasion might have sent a fitter messenger. His Holiness informs you that, at the first news of open hostilities, he sent one of his most trusted envoys to Madrid to inform his imperial majesty that he has no concern with the alliance of the Italian states. A Holy League does not exist. The chief shepherd shuns the sword."

"Hallelujah!" cried the chancellor whose brain seemed to be quite turned by his new chance of life; but Pescara replied: "Why, Guicciardini, Morone has this moment revealed to us the fact that the League was the work of his Holiness. Which is the truth?"

"Both," replied Guicciardini. "My task is fulfilled and there is an end of it." He bowed and left the room; but Bourbon, in whom Satan was astir, called after the Pope's envoy:

"Guicciardini, tell your master that I am on my way to Rome to kiss the slipper of his Truthfulness, with a following of Lutherans and converted Jews and some night I will fling my burning taper so far that his Holiness shall have light enough to see by!"

The laugh with which the scoffer ended his speech echoed sharply from the hollow dome and the corners of the hall, as though repeated by malicious demons; Guicciardini looked back terrified. The general dismissed the chancellor and his guards, either because he thought it unseemly to hold up the head of the Church to ridicule or because he was weary of the human farce.

When Guicciardini and Morone met outside the

papal envoy asked: "They are taking you to the scaffold?"

"By no means!"

"You have wriggled through once more? Invulnerable! But what happened in Novara?"

"Oh, I came home perched on an ass!—That Pescara is the Sphinx's riddle!"

"I can guess it, Chancellor, from his face. It bears the stamp of doom, and I may have a message of Death to deliver to his Holiness.— Do you remember, Girolamo, what I told you in the garden of the Vatican as to a possible last difficulty in Pescara's heart? What if my words were literally true; what if the general had met his death at Pavia, and concealed the fact; what if it were a dead man whom we have been trying to tempt?"

Morone struck his forehead: "You are right, Guicciardini! And Messer Numa Dati, the general's physician at Novara, hinted as much to me, but I did not understand him."

"It is true, then," said the Florentine. "Pescara has not deceived us. We have deceived ourselves. Oh, wisdom of man! . . . ." And with this reflection they parted.

———

There was a sense of weird gloom in the throne-

room.   The three generals, and Moncada who had
remained with them, stood far apart.   Pescara indeed,
seeming utterly exhausted, had thrown himself on the
gold brocade that was flung over the throne.   His
face was white, his breathing was laboured.   Bourbon
was lightly dancing up and down the room, his eye
keenly fixed on Moncada.   Moncada, who was leaning against a window-sill, beckoned Leyva from another bay, and whispered in his ear: " It is time."

At this moment Pescara called to Bourbon.   " Sit
down here, close to me, Charles," he gasped in a low
voice.   " Have you a paper and pencil ?"

" For God's sake, Fernando, do you note nothing ?
Your life is in danger.   Del Guasto tells me that
Leyva is suspicious — and he was whispering with
Moncada."

"Have you a paper and pencil ?" Pescara repeated.
The duke gave them to him.   After a few attempts the
general said : " My hand shakes — write for me,
Charles."

" Fernando, are you blind ?   Do not you see ? —
Moncada is moving ?"

" He will not touch me," said the general and dic-
tated in a subdued voice:

" To his Majesty, the Emperor.

" Most illustrious lord, Milan is yours.   Pescara is

faithful to his last breath.   Grant him three things as
his reward. . . ."

"I implore you, Fernando!   He is coming towards
you.   Rally yourself — we will fight them — I will call
the watch. . . ."   Bourbon was starting up, but Pescara held him back : "Write," he said : "He will not
reach me I tell you. — Where are you ? — Three
things : Your majesty, protect Sforza; Your majesty,
pardon Morone ; Your majesty, appoint the constable
to my command ! . . . ."

"He has come quite near to you!   Draw!   Where
is your sword ?"

"I will shed no more blood. . . ."

Pescara signed the letter and the pencil fell from
his hand.   With a faint cry he closed his eyes and fell
back into his friend's arms.

Moncada, who had stolen close up to them stood
amazed.

"What ails the general ?" he asked looking down
at him.   "Swooned ?"

"Dead !" wailed the duke.

"Heart-disease.   The campaign has killed him,"
said Moncada, picking up the paper which had fluttered on to the ground.   He read it, and when he
came to the third request he stood meditating.   Then,
without any change of demeanour, he gave the docu-

ment to the duke, saying: " We respect his last wish.
Your highness has only to command."

Bourbon, an exile and in bad odour, was not dangerous to Moncada's schemes; and, Pescara being
dead, even Leyva hated him less, for it was the favour
of the great captain which had stirred his envy of the
duke.

Charles de Bourbon signed to them to leave him,
and laid Pescara gently down on the gold brocade.
The palace was quite silent, even the guards at the
gates stepped softly, believing that their general was
taking his siesta at this hour, as was his custom. The
duke himself, with that loved head resting on his knees,
fell into a noon-day dream; forgetting the tragic fate
of the dead, and his own mingled lot of fame and disgrace, he was conscious simply of a deep dull pain at
the loss of his only friend.

Voices were heard at the door of the room.

" No, Madonna; he is sleeping!" del Guasto
urged, and Vittoria insisted: " Leave me, cruel man.
I must see him !"

Bourbon heard approaching footsteps — he did not
even raise his head. He laid his finger on his lips and
whispered : " Softly, Madonna. — The general is
asleep."

Vittoria came forward, close to her husband. Pescara was lying unarmed on the golden folds of the

fallen hangings. The look of set will had faded from
his features and his hair had fallen over his brow.   He
looked like a slight and youthful reaper fatigued by
harvest work and sleeping on his sheaves.

THE END.